Across the Street From the Ordinary

Don Skiles

Don Skiles 2020

Jole Street days!
Enjoy these.

 **Pelekinesis**

Across the Street From the Ordinary by Don Skiles

978-1-949790-27-6   Paperback
978-1-949790-28-3   Ebook

Cover artwork by Marian Schell

Layout and book design by Mark Givens

First Pelekinesis Printing 2020

For information:

Pelekinesis, 112 Harvard Ave #65, Claremont, CA 91711 USA

Library of Congress Cataloging-in-Publication Data

Names: Skiles, Don, 1939- author.
Title: Across the street from the ordinary / Don Skiles.
Description: Claremont : Pelekinesis, 2020.
Identifiers: LCCN 2019036519 (print) | LCCN 2019036520 (ebook) | ISBN 9781949790276 (paperback) | ISBN 9781949790283 (epub)
Subjects: LCSH: Individual differences--Fiction. | Individuality--Fiction.
Classification: LCC PS3569.K45 A6 2020 (print) | LCC PS3569.K45 (ebook) | DDC 813/.54--dc23
LC record available at https://lccn.loc.gov/2019036519
LC ebook record available at https://lccn.loc.gov/2019036520

Pelekinesis
www.pelekinesis.com

Across the Street
From the Ordinary

Don Skiles

For Glen Chesnut

Grateful acknowledgment is made to the following,
where some of these stories first appeared:

Blink-Ink   The Night Express To Marrakech

Catamaran   Iron City

Journal of Experimental Fiction   Beautiful Shirts

Over The Transom   An Occurrence on 19th Avenue, Ghost Ball, In Madrid, Midnight in Palo Alto, Origami In the Night, Some Cold War Haiku, West

ZYX   Famous, Famous, Disappearing, September, The Island

Contents

4.

1.

Iron City

In those days, so long ago now that they seem like a black and white movie, grainy and flaring, he rode a noisy diesel bus to a stop downtown in Pittsburgh and got off and walked up the hill to the college. It was actually a university, the enrollment was around six thousand or so, but it wasn't the one he had wanted to attend, not even third or fourth in the list, for that matter. But he could commute, live at home, and that proved the decision-maker.

He used to ride a streetcar out through the leafy Oakland area, where Carnegie Tech (as it was called then) and the University of Pittsburgh were, and there was the elite womens' college, Chatham, in Shadyside, but nobody like him ventured there at all. In the fall, he would see the frat men sitting out on the porches of their houses, wearing khakis and dirty white bucks, smiling; some had stylish horn-rimmed glasses, with crew cuts, buzz cuts, and he thought he would like to look like they did, and sit on the porch and bullshit, and somebody else paid the tab, wrote checks for you. What would it be like to go to college like that? On the weekends they had house parties, grilled hamburgers and hot dogs outside in the tangy fall air, and drank beer. *Iron City* (although his uncle had loudly proclaimed "Worse damn beer I ever drank."), *Duquesne* ("Have A Duke!"), *Rolling Rock*.

He had an alcoholic priest for his 8am English class.

The priest smelled of sour wine, and a deeper, older, dusty smell. His black robes made an odd swishing sound, a sort of rustle, when he entered the room and mounted the small platform where the instructor's desk was, which he always sat behind. He had never moved from it—even when they handed in their essays, they carried them to him, sitting there, with a high red flush in his sallow waxy cheeks; the veins broken and purple in his long thin nose. In the winter, the priest's nose dripped, and he had sat in fascination and discomfort, waiting for a drop to fall, or the priest to finally yank a dirty yellowed handkerchief from his sleeve and wipe it. "Disgusting, disgusting," the guy behind had muttered, several times. "Jesus!" But the priest was also somewhat hard of hearing and did not notice.

The priest gave him scrawled "B-" grades on his essays, invariably, and he wondered if he actually read them. When would he read them, for that matter? In the stone and brick building where the priests lived, off by the library, maybe in there, drinking a glass of wine and muttering, and still wiping his nose.

The college had a very good basketball team, a nationally ranked one, but he never saw any of the players and neither did anyone else he spoke to. He would go to the lounge and play Hearts with several people he knew there, for something to do, especially when it was cold and windy, up there on The Hill, as it was called, although it was also called The Bluff. It was said there had been some kind of Revolutionary War fort up there—Fort Duquesne. But there were no indications of this on the campus, at least that he could see. Maybe it was a French fort—the name Duquesne was French.

He was increasingly wondering how long he could stay at the university, because his money was dwindling and there didn't seem to be a realistic way to get more. He thought of talking to his history professor about it—he had had him to his book-strewn office, and spent over an hour talking to him, urging him to consider majoring in history. Were there scholarships in history? He hadn't asked, embarrassed at his raw need of money. The professor was somebody he deeply admired, and envied. What would it be like to live such a life? He actually knew little about him—he had graduated from a Canadian university, which was a little odd, and he once told the class there was a street in Cambridge, England, the university town, named after a branch of his family.

The professor took an interest in him, and he wondered why? The professor—Dr. Blaisdell—told him outright the second time they met in his book-strewn office (if he ever had an office, he'd want it to look just like this one, he thought) that he was extremely smart, and asked him "What are your plans?"

"I don't really have any plans…" How could he tell him that since he didn't have any money, he couldn't plan? People without money have dreams, fantasies, relief from those—but plans are out of the question. The adults he knew often talked, around the dinner table, about not getting too big for your britches, and making "big plans." They would invariably burst, like a bubble, in your face. He had to believe they knew what they were talking about, but he also had a nagging sense that there was a whole conversation, an entire way of thinking, that they simply ignored. Or did not know about. That made him uncomfortable, made him feel like a traitor to his people, his class. In any case, once you got married, the jig was up. How could you go to college and be married, have children? It was so clearly an impossibility.

"I'll tell you—you won't find what you're looking for in a bottle, or a whore's belly, either. Between her legs. A fertile ditch…" Professor Blaisdell had said with intensity.

What was he talking about? Somehow they had got on the subject of drinking, carousing? Had he made up a story to divert the man, throw him off the scent, as it were?

"I was a student once myself. Students forget that every professor before them was once where they are. In the class, in a seat, taking notes, wondering if they can pass the next exam."

That was true, no doubt. But, still, there were some significant differences. If you had to work all the time, that was one, a big one.

"I might join the service… the Air Force, I thought of that."

Blaisdell's face flushed, and he wheeled around from the window he'd been standing at, looking out. It faced the Lower Hill District, an area that few knew any real facts about, since it was a place of Negroes, none of whom—except for those playing on the nationally-ranked basketball team—came to the university. There was something very wrong about that, he knew—everybody knew—but nobody talked about it.

"Join the service! Somebody with the brains you've got? Be an *enlisted* man? Do you have any idea what that means? At all?"

His brother had been in the Marine Corps. But he had to admit that his brother was no supporter of the Corps, and in fact said, when asked about "the Corps," "I tell you what—I saw more good men broken in there than made—whatever that means." It was a heretical statement, deeply shocking to some sitting around that dinner table. But it came from a veteran, so it was hard to deal with.

Blaisdell wasn't waiting for him to reply. He often did that in class. "No—I'll tell you. For you to join the military—whatever branch—is simply a terrible waste of ability, of talent, of brains. Even if you were to be able to get a commission—are you in ROTC? Wait—of course you are, you're only a freshman."

All able-bodied males were required to take ROTC their freshman and sophomore years. "Military Science," the courses were called. They were taught by uniformed officers.

Then there was organized drill, marching, learning how to strip down a rifle blindfolded. The latter was explained as being necessary because you never knew when you might have to clean your rifle in the dark. This statement, made by a young captain to the class, had really made him wonder about its veracity—a word his philosophy professor liked to use. Was it really the case that such an event was even "likely?" He had wanted to ask the captain to specifically say how and when such an eventuality could occur, how often it was likely, but he knew this would result in the captain focusing on him from then on out. He also knew, in that class and at that time, that he was not a military type, whatever that was. He asked too many questions and needed to ask them. So in an unexpected way, the lesson had been valuable for him. He would not be one to continue on as a junior and senior in the ROTC and graduate with a commission and officer rank, and thus be able to select which branch of the military he wanted to serve in.

Blaisdell had had to prepare for an upcoming Medieval History class that day, and so their meeting had been truncated—his word. And it had been leaving that meeting, his mind swirling with a thousand different thoughts in a million different directions, that he had run into the girl he sat behind in a large lecture class in psychology. She had a beautiful neck—he was amazed at his attraction to her neck and the feelings it aroused in him. College was a obviously a place where you learned much, not just "in the class."

Her name was Mary Ann Filardi, an Italian name, he took it. She had dark black hair, worn long, and dark brown eyes. He found himself wondering if she was Catholic, if she was truly religious—then, too, there were all those rumors and myths—and they probably were myths, he thought—about "Catholic girls." Why did those exist?

"You know, if you marry one—and that's what they want, always remember that they want you to marry them!—you have to convert to *being one*. And you have to swear to raise your children as *Catholics*, too. Think of that."

He made a joke, surprising himself, talking to her, after apologizing for nearly knocking her down. "I was meeting with Dr. Blaisdell. Discussing ways to avoid the draft."

She looked solemnly at him. Mary Ann was a serious girl, he could feel that already in her young life. She took things seriously. Probably wasn't in a sorority, and certainly hadn't been a cheerleader or a majorette in high school. "No, you weren't. Blaisdell, he wouldn't advise you on evading the draft."

"Not evading—avoiding. Different things."

"Do you think we'll have to fight—the Russians? I can't think that," she said, frowning. "They are decent people. Like the Czechs." There was a big settlement of Czechs near where Mary Ann lived, in an area called "Boho Hill." They had come to work in the mills at the turn of the century, the story had it, but his mother said they were glass makers. "They make cut glass—dishes, vases. Crystal! Beautiful things." His aunt's large display cabinet was full of the stuff, he knew. Candy dishes, his brother called them.

"What about the Hungarians?" he suddenly said, and wondered why he'd said it. "The Russians invaded them, didn't they? Tanks in the streets of Budapest."

She nodded her head "I know...."

He scuffed a small pile of leaves on the walkway with his shoe. What was it that made you feel so awkward talking to some girls? He had thought of asking his older brother as he sat at the kitchen table eating limburger cheese and pickles, a disgusting combination if ever there was one. How could he eat that? But he had also picked up the intimation that there was something wrong with *him* for not liking the smelly cheese and the big pickles.

"Did you get a chance to listen to that dj?"

"The radio—yes! Porky Phillips!"

Porky Phillips was a night time disc jockey on WILY, a station emanating from the Lower Hill district. It was said to play "race" music, rhythm and blues, especially. On Phillips' show you could hear records, groups, you heard nowhere else. Some were not even in record stores, although he had heard they were available in the Lower Hill district.

"So—what did you think?" What would she think, he wondered? The music was suggestive, that was for sure. She seemed like a very nice girl. She had told him her father liked the cartoons of somebody he'd never heard of. She said they were "different," whatever that meant.

"They say a lot of it comes out of Cleveland. Detroit. Chicago. Buffalo—there's some guy up there, on after midnight, if you can pick it up… Phillips, the other day, claimed they never heard of this music out on the West Coast… and it makes me think of those places, those cities? I'd like to go there, see what it's really like."

She nodded. "It's a big country…" She sighed, and shifted her books from one arm to the other. "You wonder if you'll live here—you know, in Pittsburgh—for the rest of your life."

"There could be worse things," he said, but as soon as he'd said it, he knew it wasn't right. "I don't know—I just feel, what I'm looking for, I'm not going to find it here."

"I understand…" she said. "I feel the same thing, sometimes…"

In the earlier autumn, the campus had been a beautiful place, a kind of island in the middle of an ugly area of the city. Blaisdell had made comparisons to the medieval universities, the town and gown, in his medieval history class. In a way, it was an apt comparison.

"Maybe I'll go to San Francisco," he said, looking down towards the city in its haze. "You know what they say…"

"No, I don't know what they say," Mary Ann said a bit petulantly, not like her.

He sighed. "They say—Oscar Wilde said—that it's a curious thing, but everyone who goes missing turns up in San Francisco."

She said nothing for a while and he began to feel uneasy. He'd overstepped some kind of boundary.

"It's a long way, San Francisco. A long way away."

"Yes. It is," he said, and felt his heart contract at the thought of how far it was.

The Island

Abbotts lived up on The Island. Or so it was said. But most days he could be found wandering in the town's quiet, leafy streets, occasionally even sitting on a curb, looking about as if waiting for someone. He was invariably drunk, his clothes darkly stained, hair greasy and long, his face smudged or bruised.

How old was he? And where was his family? The Island was a long, flat piece of land on the edge of the broad Allegheny River, readily flooding if the waters rose, as they often did in the early spring especially. Those who lived on The Island remained separate from the town dwellers and in fact few people from town ventured onto The Island although it was just half a mile or so away. The only time many did was when the yearly traveling carnival came to town, in June, and sat up on the lower end of the place. The rumor was they did not have to pay to do that.

The Island was a place of disrepute. Bad things were said to happen there. People didn't associate with "somebody from The Island" unless it was somehow unavoidable. In the local schools, children from there were shunned or avoided. "He's from The Island…" was enough. In the third grade, a girl from The Island, denied a pass to go to the bathroom, stolidly marched to the waste basket and shat in it while the teacher looked on, mouth gaping.

So it was easy to believe Abbotts was from The Island.

Most of the men there were accorded to be tramps, bums, alcoholics who, from doing "odd jobs" and fishing, made enough money to buy drink. A few even trapped in the winter, or tried to. But it seemed a rule that none had regular, steady jobs. They were known for all kinds of drunken behavior and the main occupants of the tiny three-cell town lock-up were Islanders, year in, year out. "The Island Hotel," some called it.

As for the women, they were all known to be dissolute. It was held that no girl who grew up on The Island could remain a virgin beyond twelve or so. Incest and rape were said to be the rule rather than the exception, and Island "families" were an uncertain group at best. Violence was common, but the local police—the chief and two deputies—rarely went there. Islanders took care of their own business. The river provided food, and also a convenient hiding place in more ways than one. Thus dark tales were told of disappearances there; strangulations, forced drownings, weighted bodies in the dead of night. The Island was a true Gothic place.

The railroad high grade ran past one side of the place. Train crew members spoke of naked women offering themselves in windows, beckoning—"sluts," they said, twistedly. "You go up there, you'll end up in the river. Know what I mean? Back door's open, right out to it…"

On the damp cold wall of this high grade was a mark indicating the high water level of the great flood of 1936.

A thing to do was stand in the dark of that place, where water always dripped and ran in a green-black slime down the thick walls, and listen as the high-baller ran through, hurrying down to Pittsburgh late at night. *The Midnight Special*, loaded with whiskey from the big distillery. Kids would stare at each other with wide eyes. It did not always happen, but often the locomotive emitted a high-pitched, piercing shriek, as if in pain.

The train never stopped at the small platform station on top of the high grade, although they often stood there in the dark to watch it hurtle through, telling each other stories of what it would be like to be hit by the train, dragged, dismembered. "Took off both his legs... they said you couldn't recognize him... tore off his *head*, completely." For a few seconds, the deep, quiet space there in the small town night was complete, and they stood there, looking down the curving tracks after it.

The First Buck

It was out on that farm, where he walked an old dirt road, not even a back road, one nearly impassable in rainy periods or heavy snow. Late November, just before Thanksgiving.

The harvest over, corn shocks stood yellow, thick, blunt but sharp in their long, long furrows. A smoky smell in the sharp air. The fall foliage, blazing with those fantastic colors—red, orange, brown, black—that astound, against an autumn clear blue sky. Two silos stood, like sentinels, a mile or so away, on a well-groomed Amish farm. The harvest in now, some serious drinking could be settled to. A little-known fact about the Amish.

The air promised the first snowfall. And the long dark winter nights. Moonlight on fresh-fallen snow, deep quiet. Deer hunting season.

He'd walk back as the light started to darken, seeing the house already lighted, and the redone old barn off to the side. A boy he had known had run, playing, out of the top wide door of the hayloft on the second story, fell, broken his leg. A long time ago but he could see him, still, flailing in mid-air.

A fresh fire in the big old stone fireplace in the long living room, and smells of good food cooking, coffee perking. He sat to the side of the crackling fire, and it turned full dark outside the old square-paned windows. Why would anyone want to leave?

There were pheasants, and the grouse, hung for three, four days, even a week. Shot with the .410 over-and-under, or with the .20 gauge, a beautiful shotgun with engraving on the barrels and stock, carried in a game pouch stained dark with the birds' blood. The hunting jacket had shoulder patches, unlike any other jacket, and smelled like the woods, leaves, smoke, a faint smell of sweat. There was a sewn label on the inside vest pocket, a picture of a hunting dog, a good bird dog. The best of these cost ten thousand dollars, it was said. Hunters in Texas, the southwest, had them.

Around the cherry wood dinner table, where serious eating was done, stories of the apocryphal "snipe" hunt would be told, with laughter—the city rube left at night, standing with a gunny sack, waiting for the snipe to be driven into it. How long did he stand there, wait? And what then? Laughter.

A few men had hunted black bear but no one had got one. Or, for that matter, knew anyone who had, it seemed. The meat was said to be not that good. But everyone had got a buck at some time or another, and some men were vaunted, having got their deer every year without fail. Does were better, though, for meat, than a buck, especially an old, wise buck who'd been in the woods a long time. A big eight or majestic ten-point. That trophy rack. *Wheeler's Tavern,* down at the crossroads, had a room full of mounted trophy racks.

When a young boy—legal hunting age was twelve—got his first buck, the testicles were cut off and hung on a tree branch, or bush, and the young boy's face was streaked with the deer's blood. He was blooded now. How many photos there were of a smiling young boy kneeling beside his kill, holding up by the antlers the head of the dead deer. There were framed pictures like this, this pose, in uncounted homes displayed on a mantle.

In his case, things had gone differently. After several hours of walking in sharp, cold weather through various terrain, they had come on a buck, alone. This one was to be his. The first one. He stood on a small hill above where the deer stood—it was not a long shot. As instructed, he knelt smoothly, brought the .33 Remington up, and sighted. And then the deer turned his head—a six-pointer—and looked directly at him, or so it seemed. "Goddamn, boy!" somebody said. He lowered the rifle, did not fire. The man standing next to him got off a hurried shot, but the buck was gone, so quickly it was as if he had never been there. A phantom.

He had turned to the man who was looking at him, and said. "He was beautiful."

The man—tall, lean, with a weathered face, although he wasn't that old—nodded.

"I know," he said. "I know."

The next morning his stepfather drove him back home in the old black Buick. He never hunted again.

West

Midnight. The *Empire Builder* crosses into the vast plain of North Dakota. A state thinly populated, with a fierce swing in yearly temperatures; thirty below (or colder) in winter, 115 in the broiling summer The beginning of the Great Plains, the northern extremity, below Saskatchewan, Alberta, Manitoba. From there, the immense flatness stretched down into Kansas, Oklahoma, Texas, the Sonoran deserts of the Southwest and Mexico. Indian lands, and the true home where the buffalo roamed, the endless sea of grasses so high it tickled the buffaloes' bellies. A buffalo robe would keep you warm at thirty below. North Dakota extending into Montana, a long state.

This is what travels through the mind riding the *Empire Builder*. Ride the train—somehow long an anachronism. There was a day when these trains were the ultimate. The *Santa Fe Chief*, the *Twentieth Century Limited*, the *Coast Starlight*, the *City of New Orleans*, the *Wabash Cannonball*.

At one time, it was the grandest way West.

2.

When I was seven or eight, the boy who lived next door and who was slightly older—perhaps ten—announced his family was moving to Montana. Such a move struck me with amazement. Montana was as remote as India—perhaps more so. As far as I knew, it was certainly a place where there would be real cowboys, maybe even some real

Indians. In those days, we played the game of Cowboys and Indians endlessly, whooping, drawing our six-shooter cap pistols—Pop-Pop!—slapping our legs as we ran to simulate galloping a horse. We wore bandanas, like the US Cavalry. All of us had been entranced by *She Wore a Yellow Ribbon*.

The older sister of my friend was a girl morphing into a young woman, at about sixteen. She lounged on the porch swing in the soft summer heat in a two-piece swim suit, bare feet with painted toe nails, drinking Coca-Cola from a glass with ice cubes that clinked. She allowed me to sit on the swing with her. It was a giddy experience.

When the long summer days finally ended, at 9 or 9:15, and a warm dusk and then full, lush darkness settled on the small river town, sitting on that gently moving swing, close enough to her that I could feel the warmth coming from her, and smell her distinctive scent, would overwhelm me. There was a great gap in age between us, but I had maddening fantasies about her initiating me into a whole world I knew was there. She was, I was sure, aware of this well of feelings. And she was going to Montana.

"You'll meet cowboys. In Montana…" I stammered out one night.

"Cowboys?" She laughed, ran her hand down one of her impossibly smooth, tanned legs. "Would you like to be a cowboy?"

My throat was full. I wondered if I could speak. The swing squeaked lightly, that unique sound of summer.

"Maybe…" I finally got out. "I don't know…"

"There aren't any cowboys around here. Only in the movies. On tv…"

"There must be lots of them, out there."

It was as if I was conjuring up Australia, or South Africa. I nodded my head emphatically, feeling stupid. Of course there'd be lots of cowboys in Montana.

She smiled, and chuckled. "Yes… Montana is all cowboys. With those big hats on their heads." She gestured as if putting a cowboy hat on her head.

"Howdy, pardner," she said, and stuck out her hand, that she'd run down her leg. "Put 'er there!"

I was paralyzed. But I grasped her small hand—warm, solid, yet soft, smooth—and shook it up and down.

"Wanna drink?" I squeaked out, remembering countless bar scenes in Westerns.

She laughed, delighted, and grasped my hand with both of hers. "You may just be a cowboy and don't know it," she said, and quickly bent down, and kissed me on my high forehead. "Towhead."

Later that July night, I lay on my bed in the small bedroom on the top floor of our old red shingled house, right next door. I could see a light on in what I knew was "her room." I wondered what she was doing. Listening to the radio, brushing her sandy, reddish hair. Talking on the phone—girls talked on the phone a lot.

The light went out. Was she getting into her bed? Visions flashed in my head. Girls, when they got bigger, were different… like Montana, and the cowboys. I stared up in the dark of that small room, and thought I'd probably never be a cowboy.

But I might.

Some Cold War Haiku

Never did go that afternoon to meet sweet Carol for a picnic in the dark green English woods, which would have, undoubtably, resulted in forbidden fornication. A quaint phrase, today.

What AJ did with his brother's World War Two B-17 flying boots I never found out but I heard via letter he still ran the small stars and bars up the pole of the tall bunk bed, while whistling "Dixie." Look away, look away...

Frank, the black guy from Detroit, had rotated. There was no knife fight behind the barracks with Crabtree, the cracker from Tennessee, who'd bored a hole in a half penny and wore it on a chain around his neck with his dog tags.

Dominic rotated, too, back to New Jersey, but not the job in the Kotex factory. He was a draftsman for a company working on nuclear submarines, and taking night classes at Rutgers. Marlene, whose name wreathed a deep red heart tattooed on his left upper arm, married a furniture salesman before Dom's hitch was finished.

Ray Phillips got a job at Western Union and called one Sunday afternoon, chuckling as though sobbing, recalling when the punt sank right from underneath us out on the Cam.

Petersen re-upped for six more, made Staff Sergeant, got a nine hundred dollar bonus, extended his tour in England for a year, and married the beautiful daughter of a local pig farmer—a swineherd, they called them. He would be a lifer, no question. Buy a couple of gas stations, retire down in Louisiana, a Chief Master Sergeant. No further to go.

And Kyle, of all people, actually managed to pull off getting discharged in England, on the base no less. He had fallen in with some guy, a shady character to be sure, in Queensway, in London, and this guy had written a letter certifying he had a job waiting for him. "Gainful employment," Kyle said, grinning. "That's what you need, see—the Brits don't won't no bums around, unemployed and all…"

And around seven in the evening one soft night in October, the hush of dusk settling over the city, the street lights coming on, I was standing on a streetcar island at Market and Third, waiting for the L Taraval car, when somebody tapped me on the shoulder, saying "Got a light?"

It was Harmon. He'd seen me from across the crowded intersection. He was in civvies, looked heavier, muscular, and after a few minutes, he suggested we go and get a beer. Said he'd joined the paratroopers, of all things, but then he added he'd gotten a girl pregnant and it was partly due to that that he'd re-upped.

But I wanted to go home, back to my one room, with the bed behind a small screen—albeit it was a large room with bay windows, a working fireplace, with built-in bookcases on either side. I wanted to make a small fire, read some poetry, give myself up to dreaming, listening to the fire crack and snap. I was tired and I hadn't been a civilian for long.

"Where you headed?" I asked as we stood and smoked—the familiar red pack of Pall Malls. The preferred smoke. Down the tracks, in the gathering dusk, I saw the familiar green and yellow trolley swinging rapidly towards us.

"I'm shipping out, man. Over at Oakland—but I got to go up to Travis to do it. An Air Force base. They say it's up near Sacramento.""

"Yeah? Where to—Japan, Korea? Not the Philippines."

He shook his head. "Okinawa… then, Vietnam," he said, He looked around him as if he was trying to locate it, somewhere right there. "Ever hear of it?"

I started to answer, then shook my head. The clanking trolley pulled up, bell ringing; the doors slammed open. I grabbed Harmon's hand, shook it, nodded. I got up the steps, paid my fare, turned then, and looked back. The car's bell clanged loudly, it surged forward, and Harmon raised his hand, standing there on the island.

Skegness Annie

She was one of the English girls brought onto the big air-base in the Fen country, twenty miles from Cambridge, on Friday and Saturday nights, picked up by buses from a wide swath of surrounding towns and villages—Corby, Kimbolton, Wisbech, Peterborough. The custom was descended from the Hanger Dances of World War Two, actually held in a large aircraft hanger on a base. Here the GIs and the English girls, both eager, could meet in a sanctioned way. The custom had continued after the war, through the especially bleak period in England of the late forties and early fifties.

Some girls married GIs—in fact, when orientations were given to new airmen arriving to commence their three-year long tour of duty, it was always noted that seventy-five per cent of—three out of four—airmen spending a three-year tour in England would marry an English girl. The validity of this statistic, and exactly how it was arrived at, were often brought up but the enormity of the raw data staggered new arrivals. Thus, many airmen claimed one could never trust an English girl's affections. She was just looking for "a bus ticket to Boston," as the phrase had it.

This received colloquial wisdom put the girls who arrived on the weekend buses (which also took them back, around midnight) at a disadvantage. Some claimed no honest girl would consider coming on base on the buses; those who did were little better than gold-diggers, or even outright whores on the make.

There were old-timers, veterans of many assignations. Behind the Airmen's Club, where the dances took place, on the buses themselves, or up against them, a variant of the infamous "wall job" London prostitutes in particular were said to be adepts in. The "knee trembler." Some of the less-suspecting girls were even occasionally smuggled into a nearby barracks. There, among other discoveries, they would encounter a modern hot shower.

Skegness Annie was one of the veterans. He had heard about her not long after he arrived on the base, coming over on a C-47 from Germany. (He had broken his glasses on that flight and been forced to see much of the place as if through a mist for a week until he'd gotten new ones.) Some airmen joked about her knowingly, and said she'd been coming onto the base before some of the younger girls had been born.

While this probably wasn't true, Annie had some mileage on her, there wasn't any doubt. In the dark recesses of "the Club" as it was known, she could look all right, especially after a few of the cheap drinks the bar dispensed. But she had bad teeth, among other things. To her credit, many English girls shared this disadvantage. "No milk—the war, rationing," people would say knowingly. Conversely, it was Americans who sported the big, white, evenly-spaced teeth. Thus it was said you could tell an American immediately, by his teeth and his shoes. The latter were "big," and highly shined.

Skegness's name supposedly came from her coming from Skegness, a coastal town on the North Sea. Maybe it had originally been so, but the buses did not roam that far afield, at least not anymore. Nevertheless, the moniker stuck and had even become a generic for any older girl who'd seen some time on the buses, and the base. You basically wanted to steer clear of a "Skegness Annie," if you could. Once an airman learned the protocols of the scene at "the Club," this usually was the case. Annie, however, the original, returned regularly to the base. She may have gone to others, for all anyone knew. Many girls did.

2.

Across the street from the Airmen's Club was Barracks 669, whose numerical designation triggered constant guffaws and bad jokes. There was a tall, red English phone booth off to one side of the barracks and this allowed airmen to call off base, once they mastered the button-pushing logic—"Push Button A. Push Button B."—of the device, which wasn't immediately clear to a new user. "What kinda a fuckin phone is that?" said Phillips, the tallest man in the barracks; he had barely got in under the height limitation, which was supposedly six feet six inches. Phillips was so tall he had to stoop slightly to enter a barracks room door. And he suffered continually from airmen quipping "How's the air up there?" He would smile gamely and nod. He intensely disliked his pervasive nickname, "Tree."

Phillips was from Valdosta, Georgia, and had two other distinctive traits. Every morning, while whistling "Dixie," he ran a small Confederate flag up the supporting pole of his bunk-style bed and slipped on the old-style flying boots which he claimed had belonged to his much older brother, who'd flown in a B-17 from some base in England—Phillips was not sure which one, but he thought it was out of Molesworth, which wasn't too far from Alconbury—and been shot down over Germany and killed. His name was on the memorial outside Cambridge, where there were twenty thousand other names of American airmen. The thing about the boots was that they smelled bad. When someone came into the room, they invariably stopped, sniffing. "What is it that stinks in here?" they would say. But there was no possibility of getting Phillips to stop wearing the boots, or getting rid of them. None at all.

There were three men to a room in the barracks, a two-story red brick building which looked oddly like a collegiate dormitory. They had only recently been built. When they had first arrived at the old RAF Alconbury base, they'd had to stay in Nissen huts, last used to house German POWs in World War Two, several miles from the main base where the mess hall, HQs buildings, mail room, and even the bowling alley and barbershop (manned, for some reasons, by Greeks) were located.

So the new barracks were much appreciated—you could

walk to the mess hall, for one thing, picking up your mail on the way, and the rooms had Hollywood beds, not the old military issue sagging metal frame cots of the hut days. And you could also walk to "the Club" easily—and stagger back, or even crawl, as men were occasionally seen doing. He had fortunately won the draw for the single bunk in the room. His two roommates in Room 12, Vito Girardi and Phil Briggs, had the tiered double bunk, "the stack." Seeing Girardi descend from this height of a morning could be an unsettling sight. First, he lay smoking the first cigarette of the day, always a Pall Mall, grinning down. He made gestures under the covers, as if masturbating. "Heh heh…" he snickered. "Brenda's panties…"

He was looking at a wall on the opposite side of the room which was literally plastered with cut-out photos of Playmates of the Month from *Playboy*. Sergeant Evans had once on an inspection tour suggested they should remove these, but they hadn't.

"It ain't healthy for you boys…," he'd said, gesturing at the photographs, shaking his grey, grizzled crew-cut head.

These girls. All were impossibly beautiful, far from the likes of Skegness Annie. Cummins, who worked in the photo lab, said they had all been "air-brushed." "You could probably pass them in the street, not recognize them. The lighting too, that's part of it."

He had gone out with Cummins the previous week to do some shooting on the big main base runway. It had been built up, and extended at the beginning of World War Two for heavy bombardment aircraft, the B-17 particularly. The *Flying Fortress*.

"10,000 fuckin' feet…," Cummins had said, gesturing at the runway before them. "Roll, baby, roll!"

Standing at the one far end on the main base, not far from the control tower, the very long broad runway, black with tire marks, did stretch 10,000 feet. Two miles, to the far-off bank of green trees, English oaks—how long had they been there, he'd wondered.

This was the view a young, perhaps twenty or twenty-one year old, pilot of a B-17 would have had in front of his cockpit as he swung onto the runway for take-off on a mission, up into the English skies. Nine other crew with him, in the lumbering B-17, which would have had some sort of monogram painted on its nose, and a name, in quotation marks. Often, a painting of a beautiful American girl, smiling, showing a lot of glamorous leg. Pin-up style. Betty Grable was the goddess of that time.

A large number of the bomber aircrews—ten men in each Fortress—did not return from taking off down that runway. The sweep up over those English oaks at the far end, and the quilt of checkerboard fields beyond—green, brown, black, gold—was the last view they'd had of England. In Cambridge there was a pub, The Eagle, where some air crews had placed their names on the ceiling; they were still there, hadn't been removed, and sometimes while you sat by the big fire in there with a pint, looking at an English girl's fantastic legs, you'd look up and see those names. They had been the same age as you, sat where you were now sitting.

"Those Constable skies…" Cummins had said, looking up at the piled white clouds, billowing up, up. Cummins had taken him to The Fitzwilliam Museum in Cambridge where he'd seen several Constable paintings. It was beautiful, no question, although some GIs hated it, hated the place, the island, the tour. Everything. The girls coming to the club on the buses, though, that was something good. Even Skegness Annie got grudging praise.

"If ole Skegness Annie had as many sticking outta her as been in her, she'd look like a porcupine," one saying had it. Poor Annie.

Why were the girls up in Cambridge different, so different, than Skegness? Annie was more like some of the girls you encountered in the clubs in Queensway, down in London. Although young, they looked worn, and would do things like suddenly lift their blouse and put deodorant on, while sitting at a table, wearing the always-present London sunglasses. That was the thing, wearing sunglasses in the clubs. At night.

In Cambridge was Delia. She worked in a women's dress shop, where her job was to model outfits for prospective customers. But none of them would have looked like her— she was an extraordinarily beautiful girl, although whether she knew how beautiful it was hard to tell. So probably she had no idea, really, of the effect she had on a young man. When he had walked into The Kenya Coffee House across the street, with her, as they passed the first table, he'd heard somebody say "My God!"

Delia went out with the son of a Russian diplomat based in London, or so it was said, who was studying in Cambridge. But he wasn't at the university. It made no difference; many people "studied" in Cambridge. When he had first met her, in The Guild coffeehouse, sitting upstairs at a table that faced out onto the street below, she had told him the Russian was a boring guy, and the parties he took her to weren't much.

"Just getting drunk," she said, looking at the rain sliding down that window by the table. When she sat like that, with her profile to you, she was something. Like a photograph. Other than that she worked in the dress shop, he knew nothing about her, but he managed to get her to go to an afternoon movie, and sat there with her next to him in the close dark, hardly daring to breathe, cigarette smoke spiraling in the shafts of bright light thrown by the projector. His eyes watered. You could smoke in movie theaters— the cinema—in England, and everyone, it seemed, did.

When they had left the movie theater and walked slowly in what was now a light misting rain of the sort that made English girls' complexions special, he asked her if she knew of a book of sonnets, addressed to Delia.

"By Samuel Daniel," he said.

"Samuel Daniel…" she'd repeated.

"Sixteenth century English poet. They wrote sonnet cycles in those days. The poets…"

So that had been the start with Delia. She was no Skegness Annie, a girl who came on the buses. How would he get further? And what would further be? He was a GI on an air base, with what kind of prospects? One of the girls he'd briefly dated earlier had had a brother studying architecture at Cambridge. What would her family say? Many English families were not especially fond of American servicemen, although some were, and recalled the days of World War Two, the air crews. It had not been that long ago, really.

If you tried, or maybe even didn't try, there were late nights in the mist, fog and cold Fen winds that you could for a few seconds imagine you'd seen a couple of them, turning the corner, going to The Eagle. They were everywhere in the town. Alabama Ace. Paducah Stu. The Chief. Stan the Man. Phillips's brother. Fifty-mission crushes in their hats.

3.

Frank Lima was a tall, dark-skinned guy from the Motor Pool. He went to the Airmen's Club regularly, but said he tried to steer clear of "those Skegness Annie types. You know. They're just looking to get back to the States." In fact, Lima went so far as to say that no matter what he would never marry an English girl.

What Lima really wanted was to get out of the Air Force

and become a fireman in Los Angeles, which was his home. "Not really Los Angeles," he said. "El Monte... but it's part of LA, see? It's a big city, LA. People don't realize that."

Why Lima wanted so badly to be a fireman in Los Angeles seemed somewhat unclear. He was not a fireman in the Air Force, although he said he'd tried to get into that career field. He did not want to go to college—that was for sure. He felt almost as strongly about that prospect as he did about not marrying an English girl. So, what was his vision for his life? "Vision? For my life?" he had said, drinking coffee in the Snack Bar. "Get a good job, get married, get a nice house, have kids. You know. The usual."

"That's enough for you?"

"Enough? Who said anything about enough?" He scowled, and picked up his coffee. "This stuff is lousy. How can they keep making such lousy coffee?"

But then Frank Lima met Dorothy one night at the Airmen's Club. A tall, dark-haired girl from Kimbolton. She was all legs, a flowing mane of long hair, large, rich brown eyes. Frank fell hard. He sat at a table near the bar, drinking beer after beer, talking to Dorothy, falling into those eyes. Since he usually talked very little, even to other airmen, this was noticed.

"She got the hook into Frank," the bouncer, Bill Carson, who had a black belt in karate, said, nodding towards the table. "Interesting, isn't it? These girls... Ole Lima gonna take him a limey girl back to LA."

"She ain't no Skegness Annie, though…" an airman at the bar said.

"No," Carson agreed. "She isn't. I'll say that."

Would Frank marry her, then? He was due to complete his tour soon, and "rotate" back to the States. There was never any dearth of drama in the Club.

Carson said he might consider making book on it.

4.

One never knew… And what happened to Skegness Annie? Who may not even have been from Skegness, but was, as one airman put it succinctly, "Skegness."

She was not seen on the base, the famous buses, for a while, and people said "Hey! You seen Annie lately?"

But nobody had. Then, one night near Christmas, she did show up. One cold winter night, when it even snowed a bit, a rarity for that far south in England. (Carson said he had seen the Horse Guards riding in the snow in London. "Unreal," he said, shaking his head.) Then, she was gone.

She was almost a mascot for the base, and some men concerned themselves about what happened to her, asking other girls, some veterans of nearly as long a standing as Annie. But they had little besides vague rumors; plausible, implausible. She went to London where everybody eventually went. She married a bloke from a small village, an older man who was a blacksmith. She went to another base— maybe Lakenheath? Or was it Chelveston (this base had a sort of fame—it was one of the first in England, in 1942, to have American units, and the commander had been none other than the then Colonel Curtis LeMay who even then was known as "Iron Ass").

Annie vanished, with a sort of fame of her own. She wasn't an English rose, but... From time to time, somebody would say they'd seen her (or heard that she'd been seen)—in Cambridge, in Ely, in Peterborough. A few even said they weren't sure but that they hadn't seen her in the Club. She had changed her looks, her appearance. But, yeah, it was Annie. Old Skegness. She had smiled at them, knowingly; winked. And somebody said "Hey—maybe she just went back to Skegness. Ever think of that?"

Maybe.

All Along The Watchtower

"Two riders were approaching,
the wind began to howl…"

Gray. Frozen snow everywhere—the urban tundra. From the first big winter storm, right after Thanksgiving. Looked like nothing so much as Greenland, fucking blues Greenland. A buddy of mine had pulled thirteen months in the Air Force at Thule AFB; he'd sent me photographs, labeled "A Cold Day In Hell." But this was Chicago. It was December, that crazy year 1968, and "The Prince of the Electric Circuit," Jimi Hendrix, he was playing the Chicago Coliseum. Packed into winter parkas of bright colors, like Arctic explorers in a documentary, we clambered through jagged, frozen slush, the straight-edge razor wind cutting us, to hear him "sock it to Chicago!," as a famous AM disc jockey screamed out over the airwaves. The first of December, 1968… Those hard, cold streets, where you never wanted to fall. Chicago. Chicago.

I didn't want to be in Chicago. It was too big, an endless sprawl worse than LA, the weather always extreme, the people, the citizens, supposedly warm-hearted, were too hard. I wanted to sit in this classic white-tiled diner we knew out in Elmhurst and listen to the Stones' "Paint It Black" while we drank Edward Hopper coffee and waited for James Dean. Or maybe Anaïs Nin, or Henry Miller, striding like an old, reincarnated Greek god, tanned and in his jock strap, direct from Big Sur. Or Jack Kerouac. Or

William Blake, some wonderful, fey modern Blakeite, hair streaming, pointing, declaring, in the diner of America. "Behold now Leviathan, which I made with thee." They would all help us plot our getaway, they were the masters of Getaway, and we wanted to go so bad. Eliot, he was writing an essay, "With Nietzsche, in the Diner of the Midwest." Or was it Andy? No matter—we would all be famous, very soon, for time was changing. And time had come today, as the Chambers Brothers sang. A great song! The way that song opened...

Only a little while back, half a continent away—and yet already back in a different era—I'd heard Jimi Hendrix. Up in San Francisco from the Monterey Pop Festival where he set his guitar on fire with a cigarette lighter, already a legendary scene, he was playing a free gig in the Panhandle of Golden Gate Park. Everyone barefoot, it seemed, but me, even in the cold fog of summer San Francisco. Because deliverance was certain, imminent—no stopping it now, baby! Herbert Marcuse proclaimed the Millenium was already manifest in the Haight-Ashbury. It was going to be something else. "But you don't know what's goin' on, do you Mr. Jones?" Bob Dylan twanged. That was a frightening line. No one, but no one, wanted to be "Mr. Jones."

27 years old, pushing 30! Teaching at a state university outside Chicago. And there was her. First of December, last month of the year, 1968, *annus mirablis, annus horribilis*, ancient saturnalia of the Romans. She and I, winter day, in our parkas, slipping on ice-sharp slush, marching those

long, heartless stone blocks to the Chicago Coliseum. Yes, the Coliseum! I always thought, afterwards; that particular day was it. When I came down... Initially, people said it was the flu. And I thought I had the flu—the Hong Kong strain was going around that year. Nasty, virulent, it affected your head so that you couldn't sleep. The yawning young doctor in the campus clinic gave me some reds, Seconal; they didn't get me to sleep, either. But I did not care about anything as long as I was with her. It was when I was away from her that I could not sleep. That had started before the flu.

How had I found her, this magic girl of magic moments? I had been looking so long! Never thought it could happen. I have one small, crumpled photograph. In a green and black plaid Woolrich shirt, too big for her, the tail hanging out; she wears faded-out, worn soft jeans. Stands on the bottom flight of a beat-up wooden staircase. A student rooming house on the edge of the campus. Turning around, looking at me. Like the cover of that first Procol Harum album. It doesn't matter what anybody tells you, that is how it always happens. One look. You are never the same again.

We'd gone to the Coliseum earlier, in sun-splashed golden October, to hear Cream. My favorite professor, back in San Francisco, salt and pepper-bearded although only in his late thirties, looking like J P Donleavy, spoke solemnly of "Tales of Brave Ulysses" as new poetry, art. They were an art rock n' roll band, I told her as we walked on North Wells in Old Town. Jack Bruce, her favorite, wore a World

War One aviator's leather helmet on the cover of their first album, *Fresh Cream*.

Judy. A Pre-Raphaelite vision with long, lustrous, thick black hair, that pale, fine skin. Wearing a tan Air Force dress shirt, perfectly pressed in those amazing pleats the military loves, with blue A/1C stripes on it. Mine. The shirt was mine. I was an honest-to-God veteran, with four years' active duty, although few of my students could believe that. Judy—Judy Jones, a Midwestern name if there ever was one—was so beautiful people stopped in the street, stared as we went by. One man, his mouth open, he walked smack into a light pole he was looking so hard. When we went to a movie theater, it was a gauntlet. With her head down, she would walk fast; she was very shy. Earlier that bright autumn *Cream* day, we prowled a big record store in a sub-urban mall, something we loved to do almost more than anything else, but we could not have said why. After all, we were against consumerism, malls. The War. Look, we are still there, staring in awe at Hendrix's just released double album. His physical appearance as dramatic, in another, to-tally different way, as hers.

"He played in Little Richard's group, touring in Europe," I told her. "And he was in the airborne. The paratroopers. Can you believe that?" It was as outrageous a contradiction as Little Richard himself. Jimi Hendrix, a paratrooper.

She nodded slowly, solemnly. How serious, this music. It would make you free ("I Feel Free," Cream sang), freer than people had ever been—or had any right to be, my friend, my Main Man, from the West Coast, from that great city of Modesto ("the Turkey capital of the world!") down in the Central Valley, skinny Andy Hagen said, putting it to his class in freshman English, English 103. "You're fucking free, you don't even know it. Shit!" Booming it out, in the Halls of Academe! Right next door to my classroom, where I sit on the desk, rocking my black Beatles boots, wearing a black turtleneck sweater and Indian love beads, smoking one Taryeton after another, using a yellow plastic ashtray I carried in my briefcase. The class loves me so much they give me an inscribed lighter. *Mr. Thomas. Section 72. 1967.* I was becoming legendary, in my first year of teaching. Andy assigned a famous essay, Jerry Farber's "The Student As Nigger," as required reading, and so did I. Still under thirty, we were teaching in a *fucking university*, man! Shit! We were going to change things. And we weren't going back. That was part of it, what happened. There was no going back. No way. And no way out.

And Hendrix. He was the apotheosis. Of this music, the music, our ritual and myth, our bond. There were many, many acolytes. My friend Eliot, another young faculty member just hired, had gone on the campus radio station, into immediate trouble, playing a notorious album, *Dr. John, The Night Tripper*. One night earlier that magic autumn, in a small, dark woods, the moon shining brightly, Judy and I jump over a small, straight wooden branch. Three times. "Now we're married," she said. "We will always be married." I believed her. I cast the *I Ching*, wishing the Tarot reader I knew from the Coast, Betsy, was there so she could read our cards, tell us everything. I said, "Lunder and tightening!" in extremes of happiness, just walking with Judy in the evening. It did not matter where we were going. We did not *know*, and I felt so good, right, about that. Shaking with sex, smoking an after cigarette as if I would eat its fire, sure I could slay all dragons. So was she.

Judy Jones. Her prosaic, generic, all-American name. Hagen quickly swooped on that, over bad spaghetti in an off-campus diner made out of a real Burlington Line caboose, pointed out this was *the same name* as the girl in Fitzgerald's great story "Winter Dreams."

"That story. A test run. *Gatsby,* in miniature…" he'd said in between slurping his *spaghetti bologenese*. "Spag bol, the Brits call it, you know?" A single strand of spaghetti adhered to his shirt, over the pocket where a big ballpoint pen was clipped, sagging. Always had a pen on him, Hagen, always ready to make notes for the essays he would write, was writing; he would pull out a dog-eared notebook in the middle of a conversation, wherever, to get something down. He eyed me carefully. "You know, I've told you this before, Ray. In some indefinable yet definite way, you, my friend, remind me of Fitzgerald."

"Yes. I have a small dick."

Our whoops of laughter made the citizens in the diner look askance at us. We had long hair, Hagan a ponytail even, after all. Tight pants hung low on our hips, what there was of them.

I told her I would take her to Big Sur. Or we would live on the island of Rhodes, where Lawrence Durrell had lived, and have a half a dozen kids. Hell! Why not? Her eyes shone. She believed me. I was twenty seven years old. I had to do something. I would do something, it was definite, nobody knew exactly what it was but you could just tell, there was an aura about me, I was charismatic in the classroom.

At that Cream concert a young, shaggy-haired guy, passing me a toke, shook his head and said, "That is one beautiful girl, man. I mean"—suddenly tears were welling in his eyes—"she's beautiful! Damn! You know what I'm talking about? A girl that beautiful is dangerous. I mean, that is major-league! You know I'm not tryin'…"

"I know," I said, nodding spastically, choking on the rough grass. A week before, in the hazy early autumn evening, one of my students, reputed to have been a Blackstone Ranger, had dropped in on me at my apartment, given me a joint he said was laced with heroin. I had been wasted for twelve hours afterwards. What was in this one? I wondered. "Yeah. She is. I know." And I did know. But I could not do anything about it.

I would lay in my big brass bed, just like the Dylan song, and try to sleep. But it wouldn't come. And none of the music, there in the flat, helped me. It sat patiently, in LPs neatly arranged in two long, long lines along an entire wall of the flat's big front room. "Holy shit!" an amazed student would gasp, as if they had just discovered The Treasure. Everything was there—The Doors, the Dead, the Airplane (even the first album, with Signe Tole Anderson singing), Rotary Connection, Iron Butterfly, Cream. Lightnin' Hopkins and Chet Baker. Dylan, of course, and The Beatles. Donovan. "Fuckin' Donovan!" Wemyms, my old Air Force buddy, would rave over the phone from San Francisco. "He won't last!"

I was constantly plagued by endless combinatory thoughts—oh cursed gift of imagination, I raged—of the many, many, many ways I could, even should, lose her. Judy. An intense mental anguish making my body shake, in a cold sweat. Hadn't I played at love before? Wasn't that the way of it? Wasn't it the time of it? *The Love Generation*, one of my other professors at State had already published a book about us. Wasn't I one of them?

When she wasn't there, my big upstairs flat became a prison for me, a wasteland. That was one of the first things, changes, I did notice. A place only a few months ago I had felt so good about because it was quiet and close to the campus—I could walk to my classes. Walk to work! "They're fucking *paying* you to do it, man!" Wemyms wrote me from San Francisco, sending me news photos of the funeral of Hippie, a coffin toted down Haight Street, the Hare Krishna wagon nowhere in sight. Then Wemyms mailed more clippings, from the Chronicle; someone shot on the SF State campus, the bookstore torched, a professor's research notes, ten years' worth of work, thrown out his office window and then burned, while he watched. The omnious, black-helmeted figures of the TAC squad, marching in line. Some professor with a bullhorn, pleading for order. "It's all gone to shit, man!" Wemyms wrote.

It still did not take with me. I was in another place. I could watch Judy combing her long, dark hair in the rearview mirror of my powder blue Ford and be happy. So happy! I could not stand it. If only she would stay. Simultaneously—and that was the thing, you know what I mean?—somehow I knew that, like the music, she wouldn't. Couldn't. That, that was what I knew, and what the guy at the Cream concert knew. In a flash. He looked down, nodded, and down on the stage Ginger Baker in one long pull drained off a can of beer and started in on "Toad." How long could he keep it up? How long could it go on like this? The band knew it too; this is what the music said, what it really said. There comes a time, to nearly everyone, when it's clear. Nobody's sweet. Love is not going to save you.

We made our love on long smoky fall afternoons in the flat near the campus. On John Street, a prosaic, comic name in a flat town. We could faintly hear the dull roars from the football stadium, if there was a home game. "She's playing the Leg Game," said an ad tacked onto the fading flower print wallpaper in the long hall of the upstairs flat, showing a woman in a very short skirt who had the legs to play, for sure. Another poster, in this place where we lay on a real, actual big brass bed, said "Better Living Through Chemistry." The girls in this poster looked intensely happy—they would make you very happy, too—and the bearded men in the poster looked like misplaced Greek gods somehow returned from that time period, wondering what the hell was going on. Something had changed, but they did not have a clue. But that was all right.

The hallway of the flat was where the real treasures were—actual, real posters from events at the Fillmore and the Avalon Ballroom and Nourse Auditorium and the Longshoreman's Hall and Kezar Stadium. Rocky Marciano had once fought a British champion at Kezar, in another time, I told Judy, drawing on my amazing store of San Francisco trivia. Vanilla Fudge. Big Brother and the Holding Company. Moby Grape. The Jefferson Airplane. Quicksilver. They glowed, rare, exotic jewels in the dark hall, and everyone was stopped in their tracks by them... Forty people, smoking Jordanian hash on a winter's night; someone, suddenly at the outer door yelling threateningly, "Open up! Police!" Pranksters. Was that the night the great prize, The Beatles poster, Royal Albert Hall Command Performance, 1964, and signed—Yes!—disappeared?

Making love in that flat... the Korean graduate student who lived downstairs, meeting me as we checked our mailboxes grinned broadly, showing badly fixed teeth, "You have much fun." He pointed above, with his thick index finger, nodding rapidly. What could I say to him? Being with her, loving her. She was beyond description there, on that brass bed. "Do you like that?" "I like everything you do." I had had to turn away from her, with tears in my eyes, my hands shaking. That was not how it was supposed to be, how I was supposed to act. In that bedroom, in the old upstairs flat, there was a third presence in the room. Waiting.

And then, Hendrix. Jimi Hendrix finally came on stage at the Coliseum, December 1, 1968, and the atmosphere was raucous, strident, like that of a fight crowd. We were a current of energy so hard it was already unbearable. You (and he) looked out on a seething mass of people, and I wondered how Hendrix viewed this, coming on stage with his two sidemen. Like Cream, in a way, both groups having only three members yet producing a powerhouse blues sound blowing your head out, your body vibrating with it, maybe your nose would spontaneously bleed. Maybe you would combust, change, utterly.

He apologized to the audience, saying, "I hope you'll forgive us… rough edges. We haven't rehearsed in about a month…" Something to that effect. I couldn't make much of it, except that I had never heard a performer of his stature apologize at the beginning of their set. The real-live Jimi Hendrix, bathed in the intense white glow of the powerful spots, seemed a quiet, even shy man, dressed in an outrageous bright pink day-glo suit. A rock-star suit. And somehow he did not seem to belong to this ridiculous suit they had made him wear. It had been put on him, he had to be in costume, maybe they should have given him an Uncle Sam top hat, too. He had to be flamboyant. That was his rep, and he had to live up to it. As I looked down on him there, he seemed a prisoner, who had to go on with it.

He looked tired, his body posture conveyed a worked, worn-out feeling. I wondered suddenly how old he actu-

DON SKILES

ally was—all those endless nights playing with the likes of Little Richard, touring on the road, the bad food, the cheap motels and cheap booze, the speed, the pills. The women, of course. I had seen a photograph of him in a Paris hotel room, lying asleep on a bed with four or five angels, young girls. He looked "torn down," although I did not know that phrase from the great blues song at the time. I even thought he looked like a man with not much time left, a man near dying, the audience already had consumed him so much. That thought made a sharp coldness suddenly run through me. It wasn't what I'd expected at the concert of "the Prince of the Electric Circuit."

He introduced his "crazy Englishman" bass player, Noel, who had on an even more violent red suit. But he looked like he belonged in such a get-up. He was sporting an outrageous, huge pompadour of hair—exactly like an odd white man's Afro. It seemed English musicians particularly affected this hairstyle—Eric Clapton had had hair like that. It made me think of seventeenth, eighteenth-century aristocrats and their fantastic wigs. The Earl of Rochester. He was 17th century, but could have been here, he would be right at home, fit right in. Maybe Clapton *was* the Earl of Rochester.

The Experience crashed into their first pulsating number, Hendrix' guitar splitting open the cavernous cold space of the Chicago Coliseum, thunder, lightning, tornado sound. That only three people could make so much sound seemed impossible and terrible. Like a sudden summer storm in huge, rocking old trees. The audience erupted, wilder than before, manic. In the midst of it, I felt shrunken, unexpectedly sad, older than I ever had felt. Judy was there, right beside me, but far away. Something was very wrong, but I did not know what it was, and could not ask anybody. No saving grace was going to descend.

I do not remember a song they played that afternoon, December 1, 1968 (you can look it up) in Chicago. Not a single one. Did he do "Wild Thing" or "Purple Haze"—the song all the college kids loved—or the even more loved "Are You Experienced?", the one a sullen little blonde coed with heavily made-up eyes had asked me if I "knew?" Did I like it, she had said, looking at me steadily. My own favorite Hendrix piece was "All Along the Watchtower," the Bob Dylan song Hendrix covered and (I thought) improved on. His version was the one I preferred.

But I don't recall if he played that one either, and certainly I think I would. I remember, mainly, a pounding wave of sound, so loud and incessant it seemed something had to give way at any second—an instrument, or one of the players, or the thrashing, gyrating bodies pumping up and down and sideways in the aisles, in their places, on the floor; they would suddenly burst into flames, in a monumental, writhing, willing pyre. It was some rite I did not belong at, or even want to be at. (Later, I realized it reminded me of the flickering, torch-lit Hitler Nuremberg rallies—the same frenzy.) I wanted to be gone from there. I wanted it to be quiet, and I wanted to be alone. With her, in the upstairs flat fifty miles away, in an old wooden frame house.

And then, like everything must be, it was over. What do you do after something, somebody, like Jimi Hendrix? What does he do? I found the parking lot we'd parked in, far from the Coliseum, felt the heavy weight of the drive back settle down on me. The long Eisenhower Expressway roll, out of the lit-up, glowing city ("Moloch! Moloch! Moloch!," Ginsberg's poem chanted in my head), and then US 30, out straight to Elmhurst. A kaleidoscopic blur. Then, as we nearly always did, we drove by the Edward Hopper coffee shop, down near the railroad station; we parked in front of it and sat there for a bit. We did not say much, but we never really did, and did not need to. I felt drained, tired—tireder than I could remember feeling in a long, long time. Why did I suddenly feel so tired? I had been in some sort of struggle—was this Hendrix's music?

It was not far from the coffee shop to her family's small, white, suburban frame house. I had come to know and love this modest little house; it felt like I'd lived there for years. It was the house, the feelings, I'd always wanted to live in. But I lagged behind her, walking towards the door of this house that now seemed far away. And there, in that mundane moment of walking to the front door, it hit me; it hit me so hard I lurched forward, nearly falling, and she asked me if I was all right, and I lied and said it was just a patch of ice, on the sidewalk.

There would be no Getaway. We weren't going to break

free, make it out of that town, like all the songs said to do. She would not be mine. I would never marry her, despite our October ceremony in the woods. I would have to leave her. The pain of the realization, so sharp I instantly felt sick to my stomach, made me shake, panicked, about to burst into tears. I gasped in the cold night air in gulps, my breath steaming.

She would marry a solidly built man, he did not say much, he had a strong religious faith. He would never— never—know her as I had, and did. But he would probably not smoke dope, or read William Blake or Yeats or James Joyce or go to Truffaut or WC Fields films—all things I'd introduced her to. He would work hard, regularly, and come home, and eat. Watch some television... they would go to their bed, night in, night out, all that incalculable time, a lifetime, she would lie in bed and think of me—just as, somewhere, I would be thinking of her. She would never tell him; he would never know. Only we would know. And we would never see each other again.

All of this ran like a clicking night train over the rails in my mind. I felt fifty years old, heavy, a heaviness I'd never known was in me. My face had to be showing what I was feeling. But Judy was pulling on my Buchanan plaid tie— lightly, not hard, and I tried to smile, to come to.

"I like this very much," she'd said, and no sooner had she said it, than I was stripping it off, handing it, neatly folded (I hadn't been in the Air Force all those long, long four years for nothing, had I?) to her.

"It's yours. It'll always look better, on you." It would join the many other gifts I'd given to her.

Somehow I continued on down that walkway, into the living room of the small house, sat down on the sofa in that blessedly quiet living room with her. I put my head in her lap, and I was desperate and did not think any of our music would help me.

I looked at myself lying there like a detached observer might—black shirt (where had I gotten such a shirt? In London—you couldn't have bought a shirt like it in the entire Midwest), a tie (now given to Judy forever) bought in Edinburgh, earlier in the year. 29-inch waist pegged pants, black Beatle boots. I was some sort of quasi-musician—but I did not know how to play any musical instrument. No. I was an Assistant Professor, almost thirty, with a quarter-sized bald spot already at the back of my head, who wanted desperately to be hip. Like Hendrix, I was dying.

"I won't be your mother," she suddenly said, as I lay there with my head in her blue-jeaned lap. She had never said anything like that, I didn't expect it, but I thought I understood, and deserved it. Why should she?

I knew I had to get up then and drive back, maybe things would be better the next day or later in the week—but I did not want to leave her place, the house, and I thought of asking her if I could stay there that night, even as I realized I could not. It might disturb her parents, and I didn't want to disturb them in any further way. They were good people, very nice people. I was already a big enough disturbing factor in their 19-year-old daughter's life, and theirs. And what would I say in the morning? Her mother would find it strange, her father would wonder who I was really. The truth was that I did not want to leave at all. Or if I did, I wanted to take her with me. But, although it was 1968, this could still not be, in the world we actually lived in, which I knew, as I stood there, was that house.

So I began that familiar drive back in, the thirty or so miles back to that upstairs flat. It was waiting for me, I knew that, and it would be cold and chilly, especially if the old and cantankerous furnace the house's owner refused to replace had failed again to come on. Getting heavier with each mile, on that long drive back, I pulled off at a favorite spot of ours, a drive-in restaurant that looked like a ski lodge, a big A-frame building with lots of wood. And famous, large, piled-high strawberry pies. Even in the dead of winter they had these pies.

I loved them. They were a deep dream from my poverty-ridden childhood actually come true, made real, made up to me, made good to me. I would sit and look, for maybe five minutes, at the big piece of pie sitting there. In front of me. Mine. It made me happy, a simple, profound happiness, that damn pie. It made Andy Hagan, whom I'd taken there several times, talk about another "paper" he was writing, something about Milton and Melville—that was a stretch. But that was Andy, too. I had read the first page of this essay in the diner, and although I couldn't really say I understood it, I thought it was terrific. Essays being written about Neitszche! And Milton and Melville. In the Midwest! We were doing it, like Wemyms had said.

That night I sat looking at the pie, and could not eat, and before I could do anything tears were running down my face, falling, right there, on the counter. Frozen, I sat still, not even trying to get a handkerchief from my hip pocket. From far off, I heard the waitress's voice, saw her watery, smeared image in front of me, close.

"What's the matter, hon? Are you ok?"

Slowly I shook my head. "No, I'm not," I heard myself say, in a small, barely audible voice, again, as if from a distance. Because I knew –and I knew I could not tell anyone—that so many of the songs had it wrong. Very wrong.

I stood up, left the pie and a remembered tip for the kindly waitress, and walked towards the diner's big entrance door. I did not know if I could make it to the door. I could make out the stolid faces of the long-haul truckers who favored the place as I walked by them sitting there in a line on their stools at the counter. They looked straight ahead, not at me. None of them looked at me, and as I got to the door I realized no one in the place was talking; even the juke box, always playing in there, was silent.

Outside, it was cold and very dark. Out of the intense, dark bowl of the sky, light, feathery snow had begun to fall. I felt it on my face, remembered how as a kid I would stand and let snow fall on my face, my tongue stuck out. I found my car in the big parking lot somehow, and pulled out onto US 30, that old Lincoln Highway of the 1930s and 40s, now a forgotten road, overtaken by the big monster expressways, the Interstate. It represented something about the whole country, something that was happening that nobody really understood, but there was no stopping it. There were even occasional markers bearing Lincoln's image still in place along this road, like something from a much older age, Roman-like, that Americans had left as relics of their civilization, their time on the land. Hunched over the wheel, I drove in a wooden trance, my mouth hanging slack. I was shivering, although I had the car heater on full blast.

If you stayed on that road, kept going, it would take you on and on, into Iowa, Nebraska, Wyoming, the Great Plains, the real West, the dark long stretch of the Republic where the buffalo and the Indians had been slaughtered not long ago. I could drive deeper into that snow, maybe into the heart of a blizzard. If I kept going long enough, if I could keep going long enough, I would wind up in San Francisco, the city Oscar Wilde said everyone reported missing eventually turned up in. Staring into the receding darkness in front of the headlights' beams, that white line always curling out in front of you, beckoning. Come on with me.

That fresh, cold tang of the snow on my tongue, face up to it, cascading down out of an endless deep sky, laying in the snow making snow angels. That had been a long time ago, when I was a child, in another place, another country. Now, the wind was whipping up outside, small

DON SKILES

tornadoes on the road, and I could hear its whistle, a great white force, white and whiter, swirling into the darkness. I would be lucky to get back home, out of this vast night, ahead of the storm.

When I arrived back in town, it was deserted. The snow had let up somewhat—or I had driven out of it, although there were still flakes spinning down lazily. There was the predictable cop cruiser by the side of the road near where I lived. They were always out there. Now there was real talk of a narcotics squad infiltration of the student body—young cops who pretended to be students so they could make drug busts. Walking up the stairs to my flat, I felt a real jolt of fear. I did not want to go to jail in Illinois. I could imagine the livid headlines; "Professor In Drug Bust At University."

In the flat, the furnace had failed to come on once again, and it was cold. I sat limply in an old chair found in one of the many "Antique Barns" the area had—college towns always had a lot of these—and looked around the flat. There were a lot of books in the place. They were in every room, piled on the floor, by the brass bed even, on an old porcelain-topped nightstand I'd found in another antique place somewhere. In the living room they were stacked on raw wooden boards supported on painted cinder blocks, each painted a different color. Judy had liked that. She'd asked me if I had really read all these books.

I turned on my big Grundig radio, a prized possession. Arthur Godfrey was on—he had been on forever—some sort of replay from his morning show, doing his spiel for "Froot-a-the Looom!" underwear. He loved to say it, drawing it out, braying like a jackass. The total opposite of Jimi Hendrix, he represented the old generation, concerned about underwear and shoes, we were rebelling against.

When I looked into the flat dark winter night outside, a quote from Ecclesiastes came into my mind. "Vanity of vanities, saith the preacher. All is vanity." The age I was a part of, a promoter of, shilling in front of my classes in my hip togs, my incredible 29-inch waist pants, my Beatle boots, was really a dark one, full of increasingly unbridled ambition, ego, mindless style. Vanity. The head of the English Department kept a stash of dope in a hollow in an old tree a mile from his house. Was that not a measure of it? What the hell was the Head of the Department, a man his age, doing? He wanted to be hip, to be cool, at all costs; some kind of culture hero. But the Heroes themselves, they were clever—certainly, cool—liars and manipulators, composing and singing anthems denouncing the very practices—the "System"—making them wealthy beyond anyone's dreams, at a very young , unprecedented age. A professor's realization, but true nonetheless.

Hendrix, though, he was legitimate. He was not part of it, somehow, but he would not live long. It knelled in my tired head. He would not live long, he would become History, and I, I would tell teenagers to come, yet unconceived, years hence, that I, I had actually, on December 1, 1968, the day just passed, heard and seen the man himself. Jimi

Hendrix live! Their eyes would widen; I was their Ancient Mariner. I would tell them other things—of the brick of Jordanian hash, brought by two dark young men with trim moustaches and coal black gleaming eyes, that I had turned over and over in my hands, in a dank cellar flat in Earl's Court, in London. A whole fucking brick, man! A Key, a kilo! And I would tell them of my angel, Judy, Midwestern Judy, who could have posed for Burne-Jones, Rossetti, Morris. We had jumped over a stick in moonlit woods, and been married.

2.

Beautiful Shirts

At that time, I didn't have a shirt to my name. The ass was out of both pair of pants I had... like Huck Finn's father, whose hat was "like a jint of stove pipe... such a hat for a man like me to wear, one of the richest men..."

Men today—some men—wear knitted Peruvian peasant caps.

Shirt off his back, he would give you. There was a woman, young, a long time ago, living in a rented house with a hand-built stone fireplace. She wore men's shirts, too big for her (she was petite), they came down to the middle of her thighs.

British shirts. They are expensive; bespoke shirts. Half a dozen at a go. Finest Egyptian cotton. No gentleman wears a silk shirt. Same with silk sheets. The same.

Tuck it in, or leave it out?

Barrel cuff? French?

Top button undone?

Button-down collar? Or wide?

Full-cut, traditional, or slim fit?

There was a time. When men wore paisley patterned shirts, and some wore faded denim shirts with embroidered collars and cuffs, embroidered by their girl friends. Those were beautiful. (It was before tattoos.)

And that's what Daisy Buchanan said to Gatsby, isn't it?

As he threw armfuls of shirts onto the bed, a kaleidoscope of colors, autumn leaves falling, that green light glowing at the end of the dock.

"They're such beautiful shirts," Daisy said, crying.

A shirt should break expectations.

Wearing an old shirt, faded into faded, at a small scarred desk, with a glass of amber whiskey, a cup of dark coffee, and a leaky window looking out on fog, close.

Dolly out, and up.

Roll credits. Lights up.

Fucking beautiful.

Hermes Trismegistus

Tonight.

Tonight, there are writers sitting in rooms in Saigon, where Graham Greene used to be. Up in Hanoi, where two Americans smoke on a roof-top in the city and remember "the States…," like Whitman. In Hue, the Pearl River and Death.

There are writers in Denver, where Ginsberg's "NC" roamed and drove, and down in Oaxaca, and over in Mexico City, place of innumerable stories that will never be told, because Roberto Bolano is gone now.

In the brain of the Russian man in the clinic who wears a small sign around his neck "I Am 101 Years Old." Born before the Revolution, the Bolsheviks. Rasputin still alive. Now gives sign/blessing on beer bottle.

Fresh orange juice, blueberry pancakes, maple syrup, sausage links. Two eggs, sunny side up. Coffee, black. The writer who drives every morning to Sausalito with his laptop.

The old Marine combat vet, 87, Korea, forgotten war, on the bus discoursing on the virtues of the Enfield .303 and .306, which the Brits had. "Good sniper weapon…"

In an actual letter from Cleveland. "It's cold here, man, it really is. And flat…"

In Phnom Penh, eating fried spiders, Skyping. "There

are a lot of birds here. Everywhere…" In Havana, where Hemingway was, eating just-caught *dorado*, from the grill. Che's neon image huge on a building, like Mao in Beijing, where the Street of Five Rats is. The slings and arrows of outrageous fortune.

Two writers are in a convertible rolling down the highway, somewhere east of Barstow, re-creating a famous trip. One still has, and prefers, a typewriter, portable, that has traveled the proverbial Everywhere. A Hermes.

With the dog and the fire, rain pelting outside in the night, which seems old, very old. On a night like this people went to the great stone circles and women slept outside, waiting for the Cerne Abbas Giant, in Druidic Dorset.

On the ballpoint pen, writing. It reads "Japan."

Always in the coffeehouse, he looks up and says, "Just let me finish this coffee…"

The Writer

A photograph of a man walking up a steep, cobbled, wet street somewhere in Europe. The man was travelling; he carried a suitcase, but not an overly large one, and not one dragged on wheels behind him. The suitcase was part of him.

What city was he in—Paris, Prague, Rome, Budapest? What hotel, flat, room was he headed to? And where would he go next? And what would he write?

He went to Morocco before Morocco was Morocco.

The Whole Story

It was one of those grey, rainy Saturday afternoons in the city. Perfect for reading, listening to some music. A fresh fire. Coffee, alone. It was that kind of day when you wonder why you are where you are. In a city—this city.

And that's when I remembered the story.

The Fretful Porpentine

Clear. Early morning, the smell of fresh-brewed coffee, an olfactory halo. Ripe pineapple, rasher of bacon, muffin with rough cut marmalade. Bach– *Goldberg Variations*. The fog billowing outside. The fog.

Leaves. Wet with dew, fog, maybe even a little rain. A hummingbird, suddenly. There. The Mesoamericans believed they flew in other dimensions, their colors symbolizing that.

What odd, strange bird is now making that sound? Never heard that sound before. Up high, lines of fine white clouds. The day will change. That painting's different every day, all day.

The stars will be there, tonight. Stare at the fire in the small Franklin stove that heats the loft. Much too small… Stir the ashes. A lifetime of reading is processing. The server is never down. You have the password.

The various *mantras*, the internal dialogue. Sometimes he wished he could shut it off. Chatter… sticking up like hairs on end, the image of that line from *Hamlet*, describing the effect of seeing the ghost.

Like the fretful porpentine…

The Perfect Job

-for Damon Thompson

He said his favorite job was when he was a graduate student at the University of Iowa and was the night watchman in a building on campus. "The term 'security guard' didn't exist, I don't think. There were night watchmen who made their rounds. I went to work at 11pm and got off at 7am. There was a small room—a sort of office—in the basement, with a desk, couple of chairs, four-drawer file cabinet, phone. Bare bones... once an hour, I made my rounds, checked doors, windows... Used my big flashlight, you know? Walked around the outside perimeter of the building three times a night.

"Nothing ever happened. I never had to make a call, nothing like that. Oh–in winter time, I checked the furnace. In the boiler room. Warmest place on campus in those Iowa winters. Snug... It was the perfect job for a writer. Nobody bothered you, nobody called, you could write all night if you wanted to. And read! Man, you could read your head off. To your heart's content—that phrase. The list of books I read there—would make a seminar. A year-long one... I should've stayed there. I should have. It was perfect. Perfect."

Hearing him talk of this perfect job for a writer always calmed me, made me feel *better*. I delighted in the image of him in a Woolrich coat and scarf, patrolling the darkened, silent building, snow falling outside, and I liked to think of the sanity of the job, its ancient lineage. The watchman, a venerable figure.

There were no robbers in Iowa City planning a break-in, a heist. No one wanted to steal anything. The building was not going to be besieged, stormed, broken into, looted, trashed, burnt down, bombed. Nobody sought to mark it, deface it. The faculty offices, the books, the student essays, the various paraphernalia of teaching, these were intact, unviolated, safe. Safe. A limit.

So in the quiet basement, the night watchman wrote, and read, and dreamed and tried not to sleep on the job toward morning. And he got to see, day after day, day arrive, the goddess, the goddess Dawn arrive. He smoked a pipe, and when he made his outside rounds, that rich tobacco fragrance followed his passing, his passage, the reassuring glow of the flashlight winking.

Yes. I like to think of it, even now.

Origami in the Night

Alan Watts used to live—"back in the day"—on a houseboat in Sausalito. There is still a houseboat community in Sausalito, but it would be interesting to think of what Watts would make of it.

The little town at that time—we're talking the infamous sixties—was low rent, still Bohemian, meaning people who'd dropped out long before Leary's famous phrase. They made all sorts of things, acted in plays and Super 8 films, even made their own clothes, often. Evenings were spent sitting around a small old pot belly stove, like the fishermen who used to live there, drinking cheap red wine—"red biddie" or "Guinea Red," it was called. Carlo Rossi Red Mountain Burgundy. Cribari. Woodbridge jug wine. Eating pizza. Talking, talking. Talking into the small hours.

Bridgeway, the main artery of the town, runs along the famous Bay for more than a mile, coming into downtown Sausalito. The view across to the big city, San Francisco, is not as famous as it should be. It looks magical at night—the city of Saint Francis sparkling, twinkling like a giant movie set across the deep black openness of the Bay. Which, when you think of it, is pretty much what it is. People come there to play parts, roles.

"Origami in the night," a poet friend said one evening when we'd been in the No Name Bar, and strolled along it, in the soft air of Richardson Bay, the protected harbor.

"Did you know this bay is named after an Englishman?" I said. "Richardson." I was full of this kind of trivia.

"And this"—he gestured at Bridgeway—"this is *The Malecón*." I'd never been in Havana—he had—but he was a poet, definitely, and I took his word for it. Always, afterwards, I would tell people the street was *The Malecón*, and they would look at me.

There was a very famous bookstore in Sausalito in the old days, The Tides. In the Bay Area it might have been equal with City Lights. For a brief while I knew the woman who managed it. She was unique—she was one of those people you could take and sit down anywhere—even, say, Siberia—and in six weeks, two months, she would know everyone and they'd know her. And she would be running the cultural hub, the town bookstore. She was a Bohemian herself, a reader of Henry Miller, Anaïs Nin, Thomas Mann, Herman Hesse. A Fellini fan. If you were a Bohemian, of course you were a Fellini fan! I first saw the film *Black Orpheus* with her. And *Children of Paradise*, which I've always thought of as the quintessential Bohemian film. Fellini, before Fellini, in its way. And made while Paris was still occupied. If somebody doesn't like that film, there's nothing you can do.

When my poet friend and I walked along *The Malecón* that night, we talked about many things. One was whether or not people would continue to identify by what films marked their coming into fullness, or at least some sense of fullness. People did not watch films in movie theaters much anymore—they watched them at home, on DVDs, streamed on a television monitor or computer screen, or even (God help us) a smart phone screen. Did they thrill to these films in the same way? Was it even a relevant question, in an age of smart phones and tablets? Had the famous paradigm shifted?

In a way, the whole question was moot. Much of what we related to was gone, wasn't it? The Bohemians were gone, history only. Their pursuits, the reasons they gave for living as they did, these made no sense anymore, and hadn't for years. Money had triumphed, consumption was God. Thorstein Veblen had been spot on. Food was immense. Huge. In food, the authenticity the Existentialists argued about so much was found. Who could doubt these facts? "It makes me think of Chernyshevsky's *What Is To Be Done?*," my friend said, kicking a stone on the pavement into the gutter.

The fact we were discussing such subjects probably marked us as failures. Weren't these subjects you discussed passionately in college, in coffee bars, at twenty—and then, when Real Life set in, forgot?

No doubt. Something had changed. But, like that famous song, we didn't know what it was.

3.

Ghost Ball

I should say, right here, that I've never met, in person, the Japanese novelist Haruki Murakami (who, can anyone have a doubt, will win the Nobel Prize for literature one of these years, soon.) As far as that goes, I've never read any of his novels. Only excerpts. And some truly amazing shorts of his. As they say in baseball, he can bring it. Yes, indeed.

So when I said to my long-suffering wife (writers' wives— what can you say? The true saints. And what an untapped subject!) I was getting interested in Murakami, she brought up his novel *The Wind-Up Bird Chronicles*. "That's the weirdest book I ever read. Creepy. All that underground stuff... he's worse than Márquez, in his way."

She was certain Márquez's famous *One Hundred Years of Solitude* was not only the most over-rated novel you could think of, it was the most boring. Hell would be a desert island with only that book. She was quite exercised about it. I didn't know, since I hadn't read it—I had read the famous first sentence, though. I felt I never would read it after her comments.

Murakami lived in a great house in Toyko, ran daily, collected vinyl long-playing records (claimed to have over 10,000), and said he'd become a writer after an epiphany at a baseball game in Japan. It entered my febrile mind that it was unquestionable that he, Murakami, must be engaged, at some level, in writing a baseball novel. And the hero was a knuckle ball pitcher.

I've thought it over a good bit, and probably this connection came about due to seeing the film *Jiro Dreams of Sushi*. It was after seeing it that I dreamed of Murakami, in his house writing about not only the knuckle ball and all its permutations—his beautiful rare-wood desk covered with books and articles about the fabled pitch—but addressing me, saying "Write. Write of me, writing about the knuckle ball. The knuckler. " He peered intensely, leaning forward dramatically. "The *ghost* ball!"

And forthwith I saw the famous pitch on its way to me as I stood at the plate, in a sequence the Coen Brothers might have set up. R.A. Dickey, the Mets pitcher, moved on the mound, sixty feet six inches away, like an acid flashback, or one of those underwater shots, with distorted, bubbling noises. The crowd was a surf roar behind me.

The knuckle ball is thrown by grasping the baseball as if the hand was a claw, digging the fingernails into the ball. The delivery makes even a viewer in the stands wonder if they are not seeing things. The ball itself, at between 68-88 mph, travels towards the batter without revolving or spinning, making dipping, fluttering motions. Notoriously difficult for a catcher—one famously remarked that the best way to catch a knuckle ball was to wait until it stopped rolling and then pick it up—for the batter it presents a pitch impossible to track, from the very point of the pitcher's release. Another player, famous for his hitting and his 20/10 vision, said "I never want to see that thing again." Spectators near the home plate area have been known to move back up into the stands.

Definitely a subject for Murakami. I could imagine him revolving it in his mind, over and over, on one of his long runs. After all, it was an odd pitch, and he favored the odd in whatever form, and even more, it was ghostly. Ghosts are significant in Japanese art and culture in ways not fully sensed or understood by Westerners. So was the real theme of Murakami's story (or novel) the knuckle ball as Japanese culture, and America, the West, as stupefied, transfixed, lunging batter? Swinging too hard, spinning like a top as dust flew up around his feet, pounding the bat on the plate in frustration, or throwing it at the dugout, while the umpire called him out?

Of course it was. Let's get that out of the way.

The hero? Actually, a heroine (and one already existed, in reality), a Japanese professional player who was a woman trained especially to throw the knuckler. That made it even better. Murakami evoked Greek mythology, that of the goddess Athena. Baseball was warfare, by other means.

In the famous meantime, a corrupt, shady figure, one Victor Cisco, known gambler and big time operator from Fresno, the Raisin Capital of the World, was involved in the management of the young pitcher, unbeknownst to her. Cisco was also a collector and connoisseur of Japanese woodblock prints, especially the pornographic ones. He had been said to hire art thieves to steal same for his collection, willing to go to that length—and expense—for his pleasure of exclusivity. He also allegedly hired an extremely agile and already legendary teen-aged thief to repel down into a fancy car dealership in San Francisco and steal for him a black Lamborghini *Diablo*.

Then he let the kid keep it. He did. In an underground bunker-like storage locker, near Petaluma. He was apprehended by the astonished local police when he took a girl he wanted to impress for a spin in "the Lambro."

What would happen when (if) this woman knuckler came up to the majors, in America? (for that matter, was she a "woman?") No male batter could face the ignominy of wiffing at the plate to her pitches. Morale would fall. A form of baseball *hari-kari* would be introduced, practiced with a sliced down spike-like spear of a bat. Impalement.

This was only the start. Murakami knew the pitcher, from a previous existence, an earlier Toyko life, as one who "lived in the shadows," only emerging at night. She would pitch only at night. Night, that was when it got interesting; under the lights at the stadium, the knuckler got even better.

Preparing down in the deep bowels of the big stadium, the doleful catcher muttered, frowned. "Now you see it. Now you don't," he said.

Will the reader understand? The ghost ball as a metaphysical proposition in his, Murakami's, universe, even an emblem of universal significance? It was also the writer's primal, existential condition. Could he—or any writer—throw it successfully? With regularity? But not predictability. There was no bullpen for the fiction writer.

And what of Victor Cisco, you ask? There was talk, rumor. To further his project—and who knows its fuller dimensions?—he'd bought the Brooklyn Cyclones, a minor league team that played in a park at Coney Island, facing the rides. It was a deal, he said. "Threw it right past them."

Meanwhile.

"Meanwhile is what comes out of her hand when she throws. Meanwhile, baby!" Cisco said, savoring a long Cuban cigar in an office above a tire store in Fresno few knew the real business of. The smoke slowly curled from his mouth like gauze ghosts.

Midnight in Palo Alto

The Odyssey was a bar in Palo Alto (it's no longer there.) The owner sold up and moved (so it was said) to Maui, "to take long walks on the beach." It was also said he'd been a Classics major at the University of Georgia, and had a framed poster in his office of John Keats' grave in Rome— "Here lies one whose name was writ in water." I never saw that.

Midnight at The Odyssey was something, though. The place exerted a type of gravitational force field in that hour. Maybe the nearby Stanford Linear Accelerator (the SLA) had something to do with it—far-fetched, perhaps, but who knows? But at that time, people would *materialize*, the bar would start filling up. And the thing was, you never knew who would come in, or suddenly be sitting next to you. People would speak up, for the general edification. The road not taken would appear.

"What about a place called The Iliad?" somebody asked one night.

General laughter, a wave through the bar.

"And a third one—Homer's!" a regular, sitting at the bar's curved, far end added, then drained his glass. "Another libation, Sebastian, please."

Sebastian was the all-purpose barman, the utility player at all positions. He was also the nearly unknown author of a collection of short fiction, *Well Now Then There*, after the famous remark by James Dean.

Sebastian did not like being called a bartender; he preferred *mixologist*. (the regular guy had suggested *alchemist*, but Sebastian didn't like that, either.) He could prepare a dizzying list of concoctions, whatever he was called. One of his most favored was called a *Corpse Reviver #2*.

He was working his way back and forth along the famous, long Odyssey bar. It was carved of redwood, to look like a very large map of California. (What happened to it after the bar closed was an endless subject of speculation, and tale-telling.)

"Yeah… well, there's a place, a joint, up on Geary Boulevard in the city, called Would You Believe Cocktails."

"Terrible" somebody injected loudly. "The seventies. A God-awful decade, if there ever was one."

"Anybody working on a script around here?" Sebastian asked, deftly pouring what looked like (maybe) a *Corpse Reviver*. It glinted in the recessed bar lighting, and for a half second or so everyone stared at it.

"Alcohol is a venerable substance," the guy at the far end of the bar, the regular, said.

Sebastian smiled and delivered it to him, and then came slowly back up the bar. "There's this guy—a Russian, but he could be a central European, you know? A Serbian, or maybe even Bulgarian…"

"A Croat," somebody injected.

"Could be. I call him the Wine Nazi."

"Hah hah! That's damned good!" The guy he'd just served sniggered. It seemed that whatever this guy said carried through the bar, maybe an acoustical oddity of the space. Or some quality in his voice. Maybe that's why he always sat there, for that matter.

Sebastian didn't comment. "I was at Alembic the other night. Up in SF? On Haight, right there at the end of the street where it goes into Stanyan? Very high-end concept place."

"I heard…" somebody said.

"Couldn't drive back. Not drunk. Too foggy. Slept in the car. Had to see the chiropractor day afterwards, I could hardly stand up straight… Let me tell you—the cars I saw up there. A black Lamborghini Diablo. Couple of Maseratis. Two Teslas. A coral-pink Nash Rambler. Yeah. Had a sign on the back window 'Protected By Tiki Gods.' Parked right on the street, you know?"

"Did you happen to run into that guy lately, the one who wrote that book? On quantum physics, and Buddhism? Has he been in? I heard he got arrested. Tried to break down the door of his girlfriend's apartment. Right over on Chaucer Street here."

Sebastian nodded. "Oh yeah. Him. Always wears a bow tie. I lived in this place near there. On Keats. The next street over, in fact, I think it is. Couple years back, it was…"

"Time flies," the man who'd asked the question said, nodding. "*Tempus fugit.* You know, speaking of cars, there was one out front, the other side of the street, last night maybe. With Cal plates reading *Finitus.* An old vintage MGB, no less."

"Make a good name for a drink. *Finitus,*" Sebastian said. He stood in his glinting glass kingdom, smiling slightly. He could have been a medieval alchemist, with the magical array of colored bottles, rising in a pyramid behind him. An earthquake in The Odyssey would have been very bad news, and in fact was a subject of speculation in bar discussions.

"Tomorrow is guaranteed to no one," the regular at the far end intoned. "And tonight—a full moon out there." He gestured out, towards the front door.

"By the way, did you know the average house here—average, now, mind you—costs around seven hundred fifty thousand?"

Nobody said anything. Sebastian swept the bar briskly with a small red towel, then leaned forward, with his long, muscular arms stretched out on it. He had no visible tattoos (which he got asked about from time to time). Small dark sweat patches under his arms, just visible. He wore a very large, expensive-looking watch, like a magazine ad. His choice.

"This guy. On the campus FM radio? Did you hear? *Maximum Louie Louie.* Gonna play every version of 'Louie Louie' he can find, all week-end long."

One of those sudden islands of silence came in The Odyssey. There was that remarkable, familiar small sound of ice clinking in drinks.

"The full moon," the regular guy said, again, nodding.

"Suicide run," Sebastian said, and looked at his wrist watch.

The guy looked off somewhere above the assembled, up in the dark ceiling of the bar. "The epiphany is always at hand. Right around the corner, in the next room, the next coffee, the next lamb burger. At Marlowe, alone... the shiny new penny laying in the street you don't pick up. The dark trees full of summer leaf. Midnight in Prague. Berlin. Instanbul." He raised his drink, dramatically, leaning back slightly. "O countless dislocations!"

"And the night is young," somebody said immediately.

"What about Zeitgeist? Bar up on Mission? Very cool, I hear." somebody asked. The guy sitting at the end remained staring into the ceiling, then lowered his now-empty glass.

Sebastian returned to his station in front of the bottle pyramid. "There was a guy mentioned in yesterday's newspaper. French Fry. Actual name. And this woman—this was spelled with a K—Krystal Ball."

A fat guy standing at the bar, reflected weirdly in the shining large bar mirror, nodded. "Happens all the time. There was this abalone diver. Down in Morro Bay. Stole a girl from me... No! Wait! He had the same name. Same as me. Samo. Can you beat it?"

So it was. While everyone stared yet again into the distance of their drinks, or the bar mirror and the pyramid of bottles, of libations, as Sebastian called them, the guy at the far end slipped out the back door. The drifter did escape.

"Home," Sebastian said, looking down the long, curved bar. "But no Penelope."

An Occurrence on 19th Avenue

I first saw this girl holding the sign when I was driving out 19th Avenue, US 1, going south. It was neatly lettered on a piece of brownish cardboard, and read *Reject Capitalist Lies.*

Why had she selected that particular corner? Was it because of the green and brown paint, or the polished brass trim (even the ATM was brass-trimmed) of the gleaming branch of First Republic Bank, a known bank for people who needed "wealth management?" Or because a very popular branch of Starbucks was on the corner directly across the street?

A half-hour later, returning north on 19th, I saw she was gone. On a whim—and with some difficulty, due to the density of the area—I parked and went into the Starbucks. I had only seen her momentarily, but for some reason I felt sure I'd recognize her. (Of course, would someone holding up such a sign enter, patronize, a Starbucks?)

The place was crowded with that curious mix of such places. A good number of people were hunched over, staring intently at their open laptops (it looked like many had Macs). A few people were contemplating their coffee, and a few staring out the large plate glass windows at the glinting traffic flashing by.

I made an unobtrusive scan, walking as if looking for a place to sit, holding my coffee casually. There was that usual

Starbucks smell, not the great smell of freshly ground coffee (as in Blue Bottle, or Sightglass), or brewed, for that matter, but a sticky sweet sugary odor, like some kind of wet, not particularly good candy, underlaid with tones of wet socks. Whoever guides Starbucks should look into this, and even design, if necessary, a competent machine that overlays the interior with that rich, unmistakable fresh ground coffee smell. The roasting smell.

I didn't see her. Of course, she could've been in the rest room, but I determined to stay a bit, see if she did appear. You never know.

Since you can't just sit in a Starbucks and look, I dug out a paperback from my trusty bag, a book chronicling a year a man spent traveling down the Mekong River. I felt a little odd, since even now you don't see many people actually reading in Starbucks—not books, I mean. Computer screens are what are being read. These were of varying rectangular sizes, and brightness. Smart phones, Kindles, Nooks, iPads. The old laptop, even now already being pushed out by the other devices. It could not be long before some sort of subcutaneous wiring to the brain's circuitry would make all of them obsolete. You would be plugged in for good. Permanently.

As I looked around, I realized I knew of no scene in a film shot in a Starbucks—or even a Peets, for that matter. Why was that? It was an idle speculation, but many of mine were, and a number had to do with opening scenes/shots in a film. (I once heard a famous novelist say that he never began a novel until he had the last scene. The audience at the lecture had audibly gasped. I didn't believe him—after all, he was a novelist, wasn't he?)

Recently I had sketched out one from an actual occurrence at the famous Condor Club on Broadway and Columbus in North Beach. Carol Doda, the most famous of topless dancers, appeared there, opening her performances by descending on top of a piano, from the dark of the ceiling. After hours one night, the house pianist and a woman (not Carol) were making out on top of this piano; somehow they triggered the mechanism (or did somebody else?) that lifted the piano back up into the ceiling. The pianist was crushed to death. This would make a good opening scene for a San Francisco *film noir*, I was sure.

As far as that goes, so would this girl with the sign *Resist Capitalist Lies*, if I could find her. What would her story be? What would lead a young, pretty girl (all in black, so maybe she was an anarchist, which would make it even better. A walk on wet, neon streets, while the fog horns croaked, that scene, maybe with a V/O, to follow the opening, the guy on the piano) to walk around with a sign like that?

Then I saw her—where had she been in that crowded space that I'd missed her? And no sign. I spilled the remains of my *latte,* struggling up out of a *faux* brown armchair that had been sat in to the point of no return. The young guy across the glass table, laptop open, white earbuds in, frowned at me. I shook my head, mumbled "Sorry...." At least I hadn't painfully scalded myself. I had just read recently that once the dictator of the Dominican Republic, Trujillo, had kidnapped a young scholar at NYU who'd written a critical article on his regime, stripped him naked, and had him slowly lowered into a vat of boiling water.

It can be hard to exit a Starbucks, I found. Almost to the door, I collided with a large man with heavily tattooed arms carrying a *vente* (luckily, it was capped), stumbled into the door, and finally out. Moving at a pace that indicated fitness, she was already across the intersection, going past the First Republic Bank. And then the light changed.

I thought of running after her, but this particular intersection was notorious for pedestrians being hit. I had second thoughts. What would I say? "I'm writing a film script, you see..." Forget it. She might see me as another street weirdo, or an FBI informant. And where was that sign?

I turned and walked slowly back to my car, a couple of long blocks. As I reached down to open the door, I saw somebody had "keyed" it, a looping, flourished line incised into the finish, as if by a precision tool. The dark burgundy Jaguar that had been parked in front of me was gone. Nastiness. A form of urban *graffiti*, I thought. Getting behind the wheel, I decided there was nothing for it but to go back to the apartment, pull up streaming Netflix. Watch a film. Maybe an early Kurosawa *noir*, like *The Bad Sleep Well*.

A Long Take

Turin. 1909. The professor, in a long, worn, faded grey overcoat, sits in a cafe, the brass espresso machines glisten in a phalanx behind him. He coughs, his body shakes, a spasmodic cough. No one looks at him.

The police already give people castor oil. The *squadristi* are on the near horizon. They will stab people to death, in packs, as Caesar was assassinated. There is historical continuity.

The professor thinks of these things when he sits, as he is now. He cannot stop thinking. The bane, the bone, of his life. He smiles wearily, his face a lighter shade of the faded grey of his coat. Thinking, and reading. His women and his drink.

He had come to Turin in a boxcar, avoiding the railway police by sheer luck, scuttling like a limp-legged crab. At the least, they would have had their fun beating him. They had developed an expertise at it. He had heard of interrogations where they held the pistol to the prisoner's temple, slowly clicking the trigger. Men vested with the power of the State.

Turin. The North. More German than Italian, some said... the German—or was it the Swiss?—philosopher Nietzsche had been here, in this city. In 1889, in Turin, Nietzsche had suffered a break-down, embracing a horse in the street to try and prevent its being flogged by its owner, a carriage driver. It was said he was hopelessly insane... He had lived a gypsy-like life for years, moving all across Europe after having been appointed to a faculty chair at age twenty-four.

His work was being published regularly. His ideas, what he knew of them, were dangerous, he felt. There was a fatal beauty about their poetry, an intoxication, a confirmation in their transgressions. And that was their real theme, the beauty of Transgression. The invocation of the Warrior.

There were young men on the new motorcycles in Turin, an amazing sight. Beautiful, too, in a terrible way. Unmistakable. They were moving, always moving. Where? Movement is the future, some claimed. "Force! Force!" the famous orator proclaimed in the square, shaking his fist in the air.

Was Government a force, indiscriminate of man's designs? A physics, as it were? Physics was said to be the coming science, with unimaginable discoveries. Going on in Vienna, which was the real capital of Europe, in any case.

Across the broad, tree-lined street—Turin laid out finely—a bordello was doing a brisk business. Men came, and went. Men buying the bodies, the flesh, of young—and some not so young—women. Their special practices. Expertise, as it were. They held degrees in Pleasure.

But that was taking it much too far. A vice he was prone to, invariably. The curse of endless philosophizing. But Thought, Thought was action, too.

He had heard of places where women could purchase the services of men, but wondered if it were actually so. What man would not be rendered inept at such demands? That would be a potential dissertation topic for a young student. Sociology, the new field.

He had once been put up, on a prior visit to Turin, in this very bordello across the avenue. The women addressed him as "*Professore*" or "*Dotorre*." They probably knew much more than they let on. He had eaten a meal with them, even, at a sort of communal table, with local red wine, a spaghetti course, good bread, and sardines, the latter a surprise. "Spaghetti con sarde," one woman had said. "Like in Sicilia…"

Sicily. Indeed. He had been once. It was another world—older, somehow, even foreign. There was an ingrained, ancient atmosphere. Even the brilliant light was old. The people moved in it with a special rhythm, as if in a play. Light, shadows. Sicily. In Sicily, a man swore his oath grasping his testicles, or cupped them, making the sign to ward off the

Evil Eye. One never knew… It was a place of the slit throat, although the Corsicans were said to be better at that. The finely slit throat. Well done.

He himself had gone to one of the oldest universities in Europe, some said the oldest. In Bologna… One ate well in Bologna, whatever else. Bologna *il grosso*. *Il Rosse*…. There was even a spaghetti dish named after the city. But the university in Africa—West Africa—that one was said to be even older.

There was a lot of fine cut glass, large mirrors, brass frames in the café. He should have stood at the long bar, it cost more to sit—and more if you sat outside—but he was too tired. He felt tired always now, never rested, fresh. Besides, no doubt he smelled somewhat. He had not had a full bath in some time. What a luxury, a hot bath!

Later, tonight, he would speak to the textile workers, and the night after, another group. He could see their earnest, serious faces looking up at him, expectantly. Now, now—he sat in this too-expensive café. No one knew he was there; he had a vision of himself amongst the others, one of them, like in one of the new-type photographs. Someone turning the pages of a book, in the future. *Turin, 1909…* He thought of a girl he had known, before, but put that out of his head.

He knew he should not smoke, but he had two cigarettes in a crumpled pack. He took one out and lit it, exhaling slowly, stretching in his seat against the padded back behind him, stretching his head and neck.

It will be fall soon, he thought, as he drew heavily on the cigarette, looking at the angles of the shadows of the trees in the streets of Turin. They were beautiful.

A Short History of Elizabethan Drama

When he first came into the room—that first day of class, a warm, hazy fall day in September—nobody noticed him. He looked like the rest of us, except for the rep tie and sports jacket (probably from Finn's; it was good quality tweed), and even that outfit wasn't that far out of line. But then he was up front, at the small teacher's desk, facing the rest of us, opening a tan briefcase, taking out a small yellow plastic ashtray (he always took that out first), a large blue textbook (our class text, *The Complete Works of Shakespeare*, ed. GB Harrison), and several manila file folders. Out of one of these he took a stack of hand-outs, which turned out to be the class syllabus.

The guy sitting across from me looked at me, a slight frown on his face. "Is that—*he's* the instructor for this class?"

We later (and quickly) learned he was twenty-eight years old. He'd been at the university one year, teaching Freshman English, one of a huge cohort of teachers hired to teach the seemingly endless sections of this required class. Then, the week before the fall semester was due to began, the scheduled instructor, a tenured veteran of the English Department and regular Shakespeare teacher, had a heart attack. Mr. Stevens was his replacement, hand-picked by the English Department Head.

Theodore was his first name, but he was known to us as

Ted. No "Teddy" or "T." He had been married, too—that was ferreted out quickly. But whoever she was, she'd left him in the spring semester and returned to the West Coast. A rumor (one of many) had it that they had decided on separating by casting the *I Ching*. But was he *divorced*? No one knew.

Ted Stevens—Mr. Stevens, as he said, "I don't have a doctorate."—was thin, but not excessively so. Slim would be more accurate. He was prematurely balding in the back, a small, half-dollar size tonsure-like circle in his already thinning blond-reddish hair. He had a beard, which in those days was still a radical statement. But it wasn't a heavy bush, like a Russian revolutionary or Impressionist painter, a beard one would never find their way out of, a sanitary horror. No. About the second week of class, some people began to say he had a resemblance to Shakespeare himself (whose portrait was in the copious Introduction in our class text), and this was true. He found it amusing, and told us he was definitely not related.

He turned and wrote the name of the class on the board "*English 380 Introduction to Shakespeare*," his name, and his office and hours. "My office—007. It's just a coincidence." Everyone laughed, the ice was broken. He then wrote on the board "Sackerson."

"Anybody know who this was?" he asked, taking a red and white pack of Tareyton cigarettes out of his shirt pocket—he had dispensed quickly with the jacket—and tapping one out, lighting it with a slim Zippo lighter he took from his grey corduroy slacks, he exhaled a thin stream of smoke. That broke more ice, and several people leaned back in their seats, and lit up also. This was going to be good, you could tell.

"Anybody?" he asked, looking around the room slowly. "Any takers?" Several people shook their heads. One student raised a tentative hand, and Stevens pointed at him with his cigarette, nodding.

"Was it—one of the owners of Shakespeare's theater?"

Stevens smiled. "Good guess. No—that was Henslowe. Sackerson was—a bear."

That set the pattern for the class—we started out talking about a bear, a trained bear kept in a pit on the South Bank of the Thames River, near the theater where Shakespeare worked.

"He probably passed it every day—smelled it—on his way to the theater." Stevens was a walking teacher who paced, not too frantically, back and forth in front of the room. He liked to go over to the windows and look out, stand there then, and talk to us from that angle. It was a sharp teaching device in that it forced you to pay attention to where he was in the room.

By two weeks into the fall semester, with the leaves already turning, the thick ivy coloring, vividly spread out on the oldest buildings on campus, we knew we were in the hands of an already legendary teacher. A few had ventured into his office building, and sought out "007," his office. He shared it with another very young English teacher, also bearded who, report had it, had left his studies in the last year of seminary to marry.

The classroom quickly filled each class day. Everybody went to English 380 and some began to bring a friend, too. You just didn't miss one of Stevens' classes. People hurried to get to them—at one pm MWF—and even into the fourth week there was a small group doggedly trying to add the class. On Fridays the class was as full as on Mondays and Wednesdays. Always there was a sense that there was something that could happen, not to be missed. What word, or words, would he write on the blackboard, for instance? And then talk about, casually? What sonnet would he read? What off-the-road book or article or film would he refer to? He seemed a repository of all manner of lore, not just about The Bard, but the time period, and many, many other writers from it. Had he read them all? The same about the London, the England, of the 1590s, the 1600s. Once he rattled off—or rather just sort of leafed through, would be more accurate—all the English kings on either side of Elizabeth I and her successor James I, James VI of Scotland. No problem. And only twenty-eight! That same age that Shakespeare was reputed to have been when his first plays started showing up on the London stage.

"Married to a woman five years older than he was," Stevens pointed out. "He was only eighteen when they married. She was five months pregnant." Anne Hathaway.

2.

There were so many beautiful girls on campus that fall, I was in a state of permanent distraction, and almost permanent arousal. Very short skirts, almost no skirt at all; these were the fashion in 1968, and I often wondered what a teacher like Stevens did, standing in front of a class looking at all those skirts arrayed out there, the full curved, crossed legs rocking, rocking, rocking, rocking. All those swelling thighs, flashing bare, as they crossed and re-crossed their legs. It was a distracting time, although nobody then knew just how distracting. There was the constant rumor of "dope." One English professor was said to keep a stash in an old, dead tree a half mile from his house. An odd tale. Likewise, it was said that the campus was awash in "narcs," fake students who were really seeking out the users of dope, and the suppliers. The nefarious "dope ring."

But the girls. In the Shakespeare class alone, there were at least half a dozen beauties. (Even more amazing was the word that they'd sleep with you if asked them. Just asked. Times were changing.) One girl was reputed to have been a former Miss Illinois contestant, and another looked like a movie star, or what I thought one might look like—maybe a starlet. Then there was The Librarian. This was a girl who worked in the university library center; she wasn't in the Shakespeare class. I didn't know what to do about her, so I took to admiring at a distance. It seemed a foregone conclusion that such a girl would have already been taken by somebody. The ever-swirling rumor mill had it she was engaged to a Marine in Vietnam, but I saw no ring on her hand.

I lived in a ramshackle rooming house not far from the campus. It was an easy and pleasant walk, to and from classes. But I had the uncomfortable sense of not knowing what I was really doing, or what I was supposed to be doing. Maybe typical of the age and the times, but still unsettling. Was I already marked as a typical failure? What was I up to, anyway? An English major. There were many. Many.

It struck me that maybe what I wanted was right in front of me, in Mr. Stevens. Ted. What would it be like to live a life like he must be living, after all? I didn't have any real notion of what sort of money a college instructor made— and that was his rank, the lowest rank, Instructor—but it couldn't have been that bad. People whose ambition was to make money didn't become professors, anyway. And you got the summers off. Free and clear.

And being free and clear seemed to be what it was all about, everywhere, then. All the songs, all the news, all the talk, all the musing. Freedom! Stevens' job from what I could see could not have been that arduous, compared to what I had seen all around me growing up working class. The men I'd seen even as a child were old before their time, sour and bitter, and often drank too much. Only sports, or hunting, involved them in any passionate way. There was something wrong with the entire system. But I didn't know how to go about dealing with it. I was instinctively wary of just completely opting out of it, or trying to. I didn't really think that was possible.

It was a time when people had visions, and reported on them, although this could be dangerous. I saw a Pre-Raphaelite vision, walking along slowly near my place one late summer (or could you say early Autumn?) afternoon. She was standing at the foot of a staircase, in one of the old houses that students roomed in. Not too different from my place. She had long black hair, raven-black, parted in the middle, and was wearing a black and green-squared Woolrich flannel shirt that was too long, but it looked great on her. She could have just stepped out of the cover of a Procol Harum album.

3.

Ted Stevens was a film buff, as they were once called, but he was too serious about film to be just a buff. He had seen many films—constant references were thrown out in passing in the class—I'd never heard of. He knew a great deal, it appeared, about Federico Fellini's films. He thought *La Dolce Vita* one of the greatest films ever made, an assured classic fifty years down the road. He knew French films, both old and New Wave. Of course, there were many references to Shakesperian films. But it was all, in that phrase, worn easily. Not show-offy at all. He talked easily about these films, as if we all knew about them as well as he did. Because of his remarks, which I took down assiduously, I found myself at campus film events and had also started checking out things in Chicago, even though that was a hike, a long drive away. I thought about switching my major to film as I sat in the cafeteria, smoking another Taryeton, drinking another mediocre cup of coffee. (Stevens had wondered just the other day in our class about the lack of real *espresso*, even in Chicago.)

The autumn was moving on *apace*—a good Shakesperian word I'd learned. Already it was starting to get chilly at night. Jacket, sweater weather. Also good weather to stay in and read. I had started carrying around a pocket edition of *The Sonnets*, probably one of the best things I did that year. Stevens almost always read one at the beginning of our class—"There are a hundred and fifty four of them, so we won't get to them all." I waited each class to see which one he'd read. Sometimes, to confuse us, he'd read another poet, another of the Elizabethans or Jacobeans, Wyatt or Surrey or Daniel, or even a sonnet from a much later poet. In this way, we were learning a great deal just about that form, but in a painless way. It was just damned good teaching, I thought.

His dress continued, also, to intrigue. One day he came in in a black turtleneck sweater, black trousers and shoes, and blue American Indian love beads, that latter scandalizing and disgusting the guy who sat behind me, a large, thick-set, heavily perspiring, blond crew cut guy who looked like he was from the mid 1950s. He was also vintage Midwestern.

"*Love* beads. Jesus! Can you believe this guy?"

Another guy muttered "The Syndicate'll fix his ass one of these nights. Out on the road. Him and the cunt he's with."

Why was there such animosity? I wondered. Threatened sexuality? Or the desire to see him dragged in the shit, back and forth a couple of times? Get him down in the hole where the rest of us were? A Dylan song had a line like that, somewhere.

He spent one day suggesting ways of reading the plays we could carry out of the class, after we'd finished the semester. Reading them at different points in our lives. Especially when we got old.

"I mean," he said, looking off over the flat campus (what *was* he looking at?) "when you're really there. Seventy. Seventy-five." He counted it off on one hand. "Eighty… *Hamlet*, take that play. If you read just that one, every five years, it will be different each time, and you'll see that."

Then he faced us, leaning on the small desk. "Shakespeare was fifty-six when he died, in Stratford, at his home. Took to his bed and died in three days. Some say Ben Jonson poisoned him… But, by today's standards, he was middle-aged. Odd, isn't it?"

There was something different, each week, as we moved smoothly through the Comedies, Tragedies, Histories. St. Crispin's Day came. October 25th. He read us the great speech from *Henry V* and spoke of Olivier's 1944 film, and the impact that had during World War II. "Make sure," he said, finishing the class that day; it went quickly, as they often seemed to do. "Make sure. Read it, every year, on this day. If you don't read anything else, even."

That night, a Friday, I went and saw Fellini's *I Vitelloni* at the Cinema Club on campus. He'd mentioned it in class that day. And he was there with, I later found out, a history teacher, a woman older than him. But, my informant told me, "it's nothing. Not with that guy."

4.

I'd seen the Pre-Raphaelite girl a couple of times since I'd first glimpsed her in the stairwell of the rooming house. Odd, how an image like that stays with you. The over-sized men's green and black Woolrich shirt. That was a fashion statement, for that time quite a one. What was she, a freshman? From Palatine, or Wheaton, one of the towns outside Chicago, where many students came from. Once, downtown, I saw her standing outside The Egyptian movie theater, looking at a movie poster. Or so I figured. Why else would she be there?

Joe Shea, a grad student who lived downstairs in the back unit, got some powerful weed from a black student from Chicago who he said was connected to the infamous Blackstone Rangers. He also said the weed was laced with heroin. I did not partake, even though he urged it on me more than once. He liked to get wrecked and read Milton, which struck me as unusual, to say the least. Milton.

He lectured me about narcs amongst the students. "Oh

yeah. You gotta believe it. The place is paranoid." He leaned forward towards me, casting a quick glance out the apartment window, where there was nobody. Just that flat horizen. "You know the head of freshman English, that guy? I hear he keeps his stash—get this—in a hole, a fucking hole, man, in a dead tree, about a half mile from his place. No shit!"

Maybe it was all true. All of it. People had to make a living, as they say. Maybe *The Syndicate* paid them. Whoever them was. Nobody could sort it out and it seemed to come in an increasing torrent, with every day. People would look suddenly around their shoulder in the cafeteria, just drinking a coffee… Maybe it was just "getting educated."

I started to read the Shakesperian plays late at night. I liked the whole image of being in that Victorian paisley-patterned wing-back chair, with a wool rug over my lap (was I already an old man?), the soft pool of light cast by the reading lamp, knowing nobody was likely to disturb me. I could go on into the wee hours, the famous wee hours of the morning, like that. And I did. I started to use Shakespeare like the famous *I Ching*, opening the edition at random and reading out whatever lines caught my eye, seeking to find there the oracle for the relevant question or problem vexing me. There were all these characters I was beginning to love, to enthuse over, as Shea called it. Sir Toby Belch and Sir Andrew Aguecheek, in *Twelfth Night*, which I was certain I would return to and read in later life. Berowne, the hero in *Love's Labor's Lost*, sentenced "to jest a year in a hospital" before he gets the girl he loves. Falstaff, of course, and Hal, *before* he became King. And Hotspur, Percy, who says to Hal before he is killed by him, "I can no longer brook thy vanities." There were the oddities, like *Titus Andronicus*, and *Measure for Measure*. I wasn't so sure I'd return to read these later.

I was probably spending far too much time alone. I found a paperback in a used bookstore in Chicago, the cover depicting one of the old alchemists in his laboratory at night, with the moon shining in an opened casement window, and all manner of retorts, beakers, chemical vessels surrounding him, along with dusty manuscripts, piles of books. The moon shone on them. Tomes. Amongst his tomes, the scholar! I loved this image and identified with it, but I could not figure out why. Something to do with forbidden knowledge. The pursuit of the unknown. The follies of Youth. How had Stevens avoided this? Handled it all? I thought about making an appointment with him. Opening some sort of on-going, one-on-one dialogue, asking him all sorts of questions. After all, he wasn't that much older than me. But I could not bring myself to do it. I stood outside the door of his office, the famous *007*, several times, looking at the appointments list on his door, then turned away.

I decided to invite Joe Shea up for a spaghetti dinner. It was one of the few things I could actually make that wasn't too bad. I didn't want to repair with him to the local Brazier Burger, or one of the small diners we would pull into off the endless flat highway, sometimes very late at night when neither of us could sleep. These sat in a pool of white light cast by high overhead lights. They looked like they had always been there. There was little chance we would meet any students in these places, whereas at the Brazier, which was in town, you never knew. One or two might even be working there—you could hear the call singing out from the smoking back where they seared those burgers over a big charcoal pit.

"Burgers workin! Burgers workin!"

Joe and I had had many deep discussions in these diners—he liked to quip about "Nietzsche in the late night diner, deep in the Midwest…" He read Nietzsche also stoned, but somehow that seemed more apt than reading Johannes Milton. But at home, in the flat, I could control things more, and I could end the whole thing by announcing I wanted to go to bed. He had then only to descend two floors to his "bunker," as he liked to term it.

Joe came over—or up, as the case might be construed—and we duly sat and ate plates of steaming spaghetti with my *sugo* sauce (supposedly from a recipe's of Saul Bellow's) at the little wobbly formica-topped table with rust-pitted chromium legs, drinking what he called "dago red," a jug wine that was actually Carlo Rossi's Red Mountain Burgundy. Joe mentioned having a toke or two, but I did not want to. I had on a stack of jazz records that mixed nicely with the fading light. Baker, Miles Davis, Clifford Brown— all great trumpet players.

"So—what do you make now of this cat Stevens?" Joe asked after we went into the living room and sprawled on chairs, drinking *Kaulua* with our coffee. "Quite a guy, from what I hear. You know, there are stories all over the campus about that dude."

"Well—I'll tell you one thing. He's a terrific teacher. In fact, I sometimes amuse myself trying to figure out how he could possibly get better."

"I hear he starts out every class reading a sonnet?"

"Yes…"

"Well, I can tell you one thing. You won't be able to get in his class in the next semester. I wonder if they'll keep him teaching it? After all, it's an upper division class. And he's just new. He doesn't have his doctorate. And I'll tell you another thing, while I'm on a roll here. Mark my words." Shea held up a long, thin forefinger dramatically. "He won't last here long. There's something wrong with the guy, essentially wrong."

I was genuinely puzzled. "Wrong? What do you mean? Ohh—you think he's really a narc, something like that? A plant, from the Chicago or State Police? That's a reasonable idea…" I had fully picked up the narc thing, in which everyone was a potential informant of some type, if not on narcotics then on political subversion of one type or another.

"Very funny." Shea sat looking out the long picture window; we could see the big lights from the football stadium a half mile away. It was the largest structure in the town. "No, that's not it. He just does not fit. Here." He pointed out the window. "In this place. Do you think he does?" He looked intently at me.

"I don't know… I've never thought about it that way."

"And I also hear he's been dating students. A no-no. And he's, dammit, he's just *too young*! What is he, not even thirty yet?" He sat his empty glass on the military locker I used for a coffee table. "Ahh, to hell with it—I don't mean to bring you down. Let's take a walk. Wash the dirt out of our navels. As Henry Miller used to say."

You could walk a long distance in that flat town, with an occasional car honking at you; maybe students, maybe some disgruntled locals who didn't like the way you looked. That night, we walked down to the *C&NW* railroad station and looked around it. It felt like we had gone back in time to the 1940s or earlier, when the railroad was king. Chicago, the hub of the universe. But the station was empty, and looked deserted. If there had been a couple of tumbleweeds blowing past it, it would have been perfect. There were only two trains a day now, and talk was it would soon be cut back to only one.

The walk back was uneventful, too, except for a bottle thrown out of one car, which smashed satisfyingly on the pavement, accompanied by a whooping cheer from inside the car, which rode low to the road and had tinted windows.

"Jesus," Shea said. "What a place this is."

5.

I had little contact with other students in the Shakespeare class. I now think this was unfortunate, but that was the way it was. (And I don't know why, either.) But later in the term, a woman in the class—she was older, probably in her late thirties or so—stopped me outside the building where our class met. There was a look of concern on her face.

"Did you happen to notice how many cigarettes he smoked today?" She gestured back towards the classroom building.

I hadn't. Stevens always smoked in our class. I took it as part of him; in fact, I couldn't imagine him teaching and not smoking. It was essential to who he was. He was like one of the French existentialists, always with a cigarette.

"Seven! He smoked *seven* entire cigarettes. And he was lighting number eight as we left class, talking to somebody who'd come in..."

"Seven..." The class ran fifty minutes, but he often went past that limit. Still and all, that worked out to about one cigarette every seven minutes or so.

"He drank his coffee up before we were halfway through, too."

As she said this, a huge noise erupted around the corner, with the hooting of horns, and an odd, bellowing sound. It startled both of us so that we jumped.

"What the hell?" I said inadvertently. "What's that?"

Then a parade of students appeared, bearing a ceremonial stuffed ox—not a real one—and proclaiming with placards the annual Ox Roast, before the big football game coming up. They trooped past us, hooting and cavorting, lifting the fake ox over their heads on the poles they had it suspended from.

"I thought maybe they were demonstrating. Rioting. You know."

I nodded. "Yeah… so you think Stevens smokes too much?"

"No. I mean, yes. But what I really mean is that I think he's under a lot of stress. Something like that. He looks tired. And the department chair—Dr. Evans—he sat in the back of the class the other day. Did you know that? Wasn't Stevens brought in to teach this class on short notice?" Before I could respond, she went on. "And now I heard that they want him to teach a class down at the prison."

"The prison?" This was news to me. How had she found this out?

She shook her head vigorously. "Oh yes. Joliet. It's a drive from here, too. Probably a Saturday thing, or maybe at night."

Joliet Prison. I could not see Stevens in this famous, or infamous place, although I certainly had never seen it myself. It sent a chill up my spine, and I shivered involuntarily.

"I can't see him doing that. I hope he doesn't."

I blurted the words out hurriedly, without really thinking. Now it would get around—she would convey it, for sure. Maybe Stevens himself would pick it up. But I also had the strange feeling that there was something inherently wrong with the idea, for him.

Whether or not he heard about my response, I began to observe him more closely in class, and I did notice the smoking, but then hadn't he always smoked a lot? It was part of the image, almost. The intellectual professor, smoking like Jean Paul Sartre in a café (although he smoked a pipe, I think.) It all—the incessant rumors, the gossip, the talk—made me realize the baggage we all were piling on this guy, this absurdly young man teaching us what he could about the greatest writer in the English language. Maybe it wasn't as easy as he made it look.

By a week or so past the mid-term of that semester, I'd read all the plays at least once, and listened to most of them. I saw an Orson Welles film in Chicago, *Chimes at Midnight*, a clever conflation of the *Henry IV* plays. I pored over the college catalog to see if there was any follow-up course listed that perhaps would be offered in the spring, but I couldn't see any "Shakespeare II" or "Advanced Shakespeare." What I really wanted was something like "Further Discussions on Shakespeare." Something like that. Or maybe a class just focused on *one* play. A better university would have offered *something*. And not just at a Graduate school level.

I saw the Pre-Raphaelite girl a couple of times walking around the campus; once sitting in the cafeteria with her friend, a tall, willowy girl who was probably the same age—maybe they were high school classmates. The more I thought about her, the more I thought she did resemble the women in Rossetti's and Hunt's paintings—a sort of Jane Morris look-alike. Maybe they all had been in love with Jane Morris. I wouldn't have blamed them.

You could hear Procol Harum's music coming from dorm rooms often—the song that was to become an icon in itself, "A Whiter Shade of Pale," particularly, but "Salty Dog" had its partisans, too. There were too many bands to keep track of, a dizzying proliferation. Shea raved about a concert he went to in Chicago, Cream and The Mothers of Invention. As he often did, he vowed such a concert would never be heard again. "The fuckin' *Mothers*, man!" he said, raising his arms, looking skyward as if they were up there somewhere even at the moment.

I did well on the Shakespeare mid-term. Stevens, in a quick, scrawly, surprisingly thick hand, appended a kind note in the back of the Blue Book. "Your answers are perceptive, insightful, show an engagement with Shakespeare that will work out well for you, I think. I enjoyed reading your exam here." I wondered if he meant it, if he even knew who I was. Of course he didn't, not really—there were something like 46 people in the class—but still and all it elevated me for a few days.

Winter was coming on, and I dreaded this. Winters in the Midwest are long, bleak, some would (justifiably, I think) say brutal. A cold night in December or January, trying to change a tire on an icy Chicago street—there can't be too many things worse than that. It had taken Joe Shea and I over an hour to do it, going repeatedly into a nearby laundromat to warm our hands. And it would be a long, long time until spring. Shea told a story about an instructor who'd broken down on a back road and suffered frostbite on his ears and nose before he got to a farmhouse for help. "You gotta keep stuff in the car at all times," he counseled. "This cold can be lethal."

So I patched together a sort of stop-gap for my lack of a social life by going to things on campus. The campus poet, a recognized Zen practitioner and translator who'd studied at the Sorbonne among other places, gave a good reading, sparsely attended. A black nationalist came to the campus, and stood on the stage flanked by glowering guards in jump suits and dark sunglasses. And there were the events of the Cinema Club, where I saw another Fellini film, an early one, called *The White Sheik*, and two Jean Renoir classics, *Rules of the Game* and *Grand Illusion*. I was getting a real education at the Cinema Club, for a quarter a film. The Pre-Raphaelite girl showed up at one of the Jean Renoir showings, *sans* her lanky girlfriend. But she was gone by the time most of us were just stretching and getting up after the film. I wondered how old she was—18, 19? It was frightening to think of the number of girls that young let loose on a campus like the one I was on.

Stevens' teaching, if anything, remained what the British

term brilliant. You could never know what he might come up with. He was a master of what he called the aside, which was of course prominent in Shakespeare's works.

"Marlowe—stabbed in the eye, in a tavern in Deptford, way out of London then... how does that feel? Frizer, and Skeres—or maybe another, who gets away clean? A set-up? A spy novel, or film, today..."

"The Earl of Essex. Elizabeth's lover? He farts audibly while making his *congee* to the Queen (Stevens made the low, elaborated bowing motion in front of us), leaves the court for seven years. When he returns, Elizabeth says 'My lord, I had forgot the fart.'"

"And Queen Elizabeth's make-up. Check that out, sometime..."

"In Tolstoy's Russia, people who wished visitors of an evening left the light in their porch vestibule lit."

"There's a great stage direction in *The Winter's Tale*. A famous one." Writing then on the board, "Exit, pursued by a bear."

Reading what he said, with obvious feeling, was his favorite sonnet, *73*.

And his instructions: "Remember. Every college, university—huge, middling, small—needs a Shakesperian. And a Chaucerian."

It all made you not just think, but experience—different vibrations in a held wire. On one day, Stevens spent the entire class playing recordings of madrigals and some of the compositions of John Blow, a noted composer of the time. We got to hear a countertenor singing songs of the era, Stevens noting to us that a gentleman of that time, among his accomplishments, was supposed to be able to sing acceptably.

"Kafka left his papers to Max Brod with instructions to destroy them, which Brod didn't. Where are Shakespeare's papers?" He turned and looked at us (he'd been writing on the long, smeared chalk board). "Think of that. Someone finds them… Maybe it'll be one of you."

He gave us so much to think about, in addition to the considerable pleasure of listening to him reading the text (some speculated he'd trained as a Shakesperian actor, that that was really what he was, wanted to be). I walked back to my small apartment, which waited empty, now getting chilly since the landlord was niggardly with the furnace settings, scuffing piles of leaves, smelling that familiar, somehow emotionally moving sharp, acrid smoke of leaves being burned, and thought how amazing Ted Stevens was. Could I ever do anything remotely like what he was doing? At twenty-eight?

6.

And then, he was gone. The semester was winding up (or down, depending on how you looked at it), there had been a couple of hard freezes, snow was spitting in the air. "The Hawk," the dreaded North wind down out of Canada, was flying hard. Walking to class was getting tough.

Stevens was gone. The news spread on the campus like the proverbial wildfire. I was sitting in the cafeteria, my hands cradling a large cup of steaming coffee, eating a donut, when I heard another student at the table say it.

"Did a bunk... teaches the Shakespeare class, that one?"

"No shit? You're kidding."

The student, who had a winter Navy watch cap on, shook his head. "Nope. Just like Ambrose Bierce." He leaned back a bit in his chair. "In fact, I bet anything he's halfway or better down to Mexico, right now."

The other student's mouth gaped. "Goddamn! These fuckin' professors."

The other student nodded sagely. "O yeah. Hey, that isn't the best. I hear he split with this chick? A *student*. How about that? Matter of fact, the said chick lives in this rooming house not far from us. Kind of a hippy type? Woolrich shirts? Very long dark hair. Beautiful, really. Mysterious looking. "

His disappearance, which apparently, from what I could piece together later, happened on a cold Tuesday night when it was claimed he was taken to O'Hare by his office mate and his wife, was a visceral shock. I discounted the story of the girl, putting it down to the rapidly growing apocrypha around the whole incident. Then I heard, from several in the class itself, that Stevens had come down with a particularly virulent form of terrible flu making the rounds, and that was why he was gone. It had aggravated an already existing lung condition. And all that smoking. Then, I heard he didn't want to teach the class at Joliet, that had been it. I thought about going in and questioning his office mate, who I'd heard was a kindly guy, but I knew I wouldn't get anywhere. The owlish-looking Assistant Professor, Dr. Krebs, who replaced him had nothing to say about when Mr. Stevens would return. Or if he would.

The rumors proliferated. After a spell of illness myself—I copped to "the flu"—I walked around the campus, now white with the first real snows, hunched over, coughing. As a week passed into a month, and it became clear he would not be back, I felt loss, disorientation, a gap. Something I'd counted on had been removed, was gone.

Later—that pregnant later—in the beer garden/bar where the perky waitresses always smiled their kilowatt smiles, in the cafeteria with the famous bottomless cup of coffee, at a smoky party, somebody was certain they'd seen him, twice, in Old Town, on North Wells. Somebody else, on a trip to New York, said they'd run into him in a deli in the East Village, but he had left hurriedly before they had time to talk to him. One of the co-eds from the class in the fall reportedly got a late, late night phone call; she was sure it was his voice. He said, among other things, he was sorry. I used to hope for a letter, the famous one out of the blue, totally unreasonable. Why should he write to me?

The winter was grey, leaden, heavy, and although it was often bitterly cold, I took long, solitary walks around the campus, while the world turned white yet again, and the small campus lake froze. I walked over the campus one night when it was like that, the wind down mercifully, a campus police car stopping to ask "If everything was all right." A pregnant question. The thick-set officers looked generic, the two of them warm in the green glowing cockpit of their cruiser. One wore a padded woolen hat of a type I associated with the Korean War, already forgotten. They nodded, and drove on slowly.

I finally walked all the way to that old brick building where we'd met, for half a year, and looked up at the dark squares of windows where the classroom was. Snow started again, light, spiraling down out of that black night sky, brushing my face. On the way back to my place, I passed a lone student, out late like me, moving easily with large strides, a book gripped under his arm; he nodded when I spoke.

I suddenly wondered if Shakespeare had ever walked through London in the snow? Back from The Globe, after a performance? Or The Blackfriairs, where they performed at night sometimes, by torchlight, tapers? He would've passed many, daily, in the teeming streets of the South Bank, although it was dangerous to walk at night in those unlit streets. Maybe hearing the bear Sackerson, growling in his pit, the clank of his chain. Now, four hundred years later, walking on land where only a few Indians had walked when he was in London, I was thinking of him. Old Will. Old Shakespeare. "The onely Shake-scene in a countrey…"

As I trudged in the squeaking new snow, I thought of Stevens. He'd touched everybody in that class, at some point. I knew I would never forget him, or the Shakespeare class. None of us would. I was sure of that. Late on a winter evening, in the future sometime, logs burning in a fireplace, maybe in a pleasant bar, or sitting in a kitchen drinking coffee, somebody would say "I remember this guy. He was my Shakespeare teacher, back in college..." He had been our Shakespeare teacher, like no other. *This is what you are looking for. I have it right here.*

And he did.

4.

The Night Express To Marrakech

Jack Kerouac. In a dismal, seedy, run-down fire-trap flop-house south of Market. San Francisco. The Jessie Street Hotel, off Third Street. Unshaven, dirty white undershirt, drinking cheap jug wine, he looks out a fourth-floor grimy windowpane. On the city of Saint Francis.

No one knows he is there.

Singapore

Come up early from fishing in Buffalo Creek in the cool of the evening, the lightning bugs flashing neon green in the long, dark backyards of the Lower End. Up the rickety wooden back stairs, in the clattering screen door which always seemed to slam with a will of its own, and open the refrigerator. Pour a mint iced tea, beaded cold tall glass.

His brother, ten years older, graduated from high school and working already a "steady job," sat at the wooden kitchen table, half in shadow, eating long, large dill pickles and limburger cheese, a combination he was famous for. No one else could, or would, eat these foods.

Later in the summer evening, the town grew even stiller, if that was possible, and sitting on the high front porch, they listened to the great chorus of insects from down by the creek grow louder, rising in a steady, thrumming volume, a sound he would always connect with high summer. Just as he connected the unmistakable rasp of the cicada— the locust—with the coming of autumn.

Not yet out of high school, he and his best friend, Paul Jankowski, often would also sit in the backyard, smoking Robert Burns cigarillos, feeling adult, talking, fantasizing about the incredible beauty of girls in shorts. Or at the swimming pool. With those summer-tanned legs. Talking of shipping out to Singapore or even India, places unimaginably distant. Maybe they would take to the rails, jumping freight trains, like hobos, a class of men that still existed, although nearly extinct. His mother had always said "A hobo'll work, but a bum won't. That's the basic difference."

When they told of their plans to "ship out" to their history teacher, Mr. Marshall, who already had white hair, he listened, head down, nodding. Then he advised them against the plan. "It's a classic," he said. "But let me say this. If you're asking me, my advice is simple. Three words. Go to college."

"But Singapore!" he had protested then. Why Singapore, he did not really know. It just sounded about as far away as you could get. Somebody who'd been to Singapore would indeed be somebody who'd seen the world.

Mr. Marshall nodded. "Yes. Singapore… Tell you what— it'll still be there when you graduate from college. You can go then."

In Madrid

This happened some years ago, in Madrid.

Early evening, a bar not far off the *Gran Via*. A young man, not more than twenty one or two, enters the bar, looking around uncertainly. Almost certainly an American, probably an American serviceman, from the big base out of town, Torrejón, because his hair is cut short and his clothes are not European. Particularly his shoes.

The place is large, with a long, high beautifully polished wooden bar running nearly the length of the wide room, which also has a number of comfortable looking chairs grouped around tables, near the bar. A wide aisle leads from the door directly to the bar. There are few patrons at this hour of the evening, not yet nine. Nothing happens in Madrid before 10pm, but the young man, who is an American serviceman, but not stationed at Torrejón, does not yet know this about the city, or Spain, for that matter.

Nearly at one end of the bar an older man is reading a newspaper and leisurely drinking a cup of coffee—a *copita*; there is a small glass of amber-colored liquor next to the cup. Two other men are sitting next to each other closer to the middle of the bar, where the clear entrance pathway joins it; they are smoking cigarettes and talking in an intent way, occasionally looking out to the street—perhaps expecting someone to arrive, a friend. Near the other end of the bar, almost in a symmetry that could have been staged for a film shoot, a man in a light colored suit is sitting turned away from the bar half-way, drinking a beer. He has a thin pencil line moustache, dark skin. He notices the young man as soon as he enters the bar.

It is early October. Not cold, but a jacket feels good, and the young man himself is wearing a good suit, dark grey, that fits him well; while not necessarily an expensive garment, it is tasteful, of obvious good quality. His tie is a reserved blue and red paisley pattern, tied in a single, careful knot. When he is hesitating, looking around the bar more carefully a second time, he is glad he has the suit on, for the bar looks on the expensive side, like a very good hotel bar. But, as he has already discovered, nothing is expensive in the sense he would think it so. The evening before, he had a seven course dinner, with a good wine, for the equivalent of two dollars. A taxi anywhere in the city costs a quarter. This being the case, he is wondering how much the various women he has seen in the bars, in all the bars, cost. The first bar he had entered, on the *Gran Via* itself, had so many women in it he had at first had a sense of unreality. For they were pretty, these women, and some were simply beautiful. Yet it was clear that they were available.

He had lost his virginity earlier that year in *Place Pigalle*, in Paris, with a young woman who took him to a small room upstairs, above a crowded bar. He had not had enough money, though, and after a momentary, upsetting flash of anger she had accepted *in leiu* his cigarette lighter, a slim, silver Ronson, which gave a perfect tip of flame for a cigarette, and had a satisfying weight in the hand.

Later, he had wondered where the young woman had come from. Not Paris, he was fairly sure. No—some rural place in France, perhaps over to the west, where the big base at Toul was. And he was fairly sure, just fairly, that she had not been with many men yet, because she was tight. She had also kept her stockings on, something he had seen in photographs in the magazines that circulated in the barracks, back on the base in England. There seemed to be an unending supply of these. "A tight fit, eh mate?" the old bloke janitor had said, grinning, showing blackened stumps of teeth, as he leafed through one of them. He had been to France himself, in World War I. After returning from that, he had never left the small village he still lived in, never going much further than he could bicycle. When his wallet was stolen, the men got up a collection for him, which brought tears to his eyes. Old Pops, they called him.

He had wondered if the girl would remember him, but thought it not likely. Except for the Ronson lighter. As long as she had that, she'd recall the young American who'd paid with that, supplementing the cash he had. He would remember her. And not only that, but all his life. As he had sat drinking a coffee in a place near the bar where he'd met her, he thought that even as an old man, he would recall her. And yet he'd never see her again.

"There are only two kinds of women in Spain," a guy at

the transit barracks had said, combing his dark hair in the shower room. "You'll see… there are the whores, and there are plenty of them, and there are the good girls, and you won't get close to any of those, let me tell you."

There had been whores—a terrible word, somehow, very accurate—in North Africa, but you were warned about that. And there were some odd diseases there, too. In fact, unbelievable things went on there. There was said to be a famous place, out in the desert, *The Sphinx*, where women did unbelievable acts. One of the airmen had a card which he showed him. And told him of a petty officer in the Navy, in Port Lyautey, who'd ended up with his balls cut off and sewn in his mouth. Could that really be true? The man swore it was true. "In this place, lemme tell you, anything—and I mean anything—can happen. And does happen. So, be careful if you go into town… and whatever you do, don't go near the *casbah*. You might not come out again." He had stayed on the base the entire four days he'd been there, wondering off and on what was served by the act perpetrated on the petty officer. Was it simply cruelty, or some kind of revenge?

Now, in the bar on the *Gran Via*, as he sat there wondering what he was doing in Madrid, Spain, and if in fact he was really there, a woman had entered and moved swiftly to the bar. She was an older woman, he was sure of that, but not that much older. But she was noticeably good looking. Like a movie star, come to life.

She seemed to fit naturally in the place, with the large gilded mirrors, the ranks of bottles behind the high bar, the smoky atmosphere that was not dark or light. She radiated energy, even power, and as he looked at her she swung around and looked at him. He quickly averted his eyes, and took a slug of his whiskey. Bourbon, for courage. He had an unsettling feeling in the pit of his stomach that this woman was going to come over to where he was sitting, and wondered what he would do.

She would walk over to where he was sitting (he could already hear the steady click of her high heels), looking steadily at him and smiling, shake her mane of very dark lustrous hair—after all, she already knew everything, didn't she?—sit next to him, take a cigarette out of her handbag. He would light it, and she would order a drink from the bartender who was already standing there, waiting. He had a pencil-thin moustache, and said "Señor?"

They would finish their drinks, not saying much, and then go out to the street and get a cab. She would take him to a sort of faceless hotel, an even more faceless room. She would take off her clothes, as he sat on the bed watching.

And later, as he rode back alone in a taxi to near where they had taken the first one, he thought about what he would tell his friends, his buddies, about the evening. "I met this fantastic looking woman. A whore, but still. I'm telling you…"

But as he looked out the window of the taxi at the lights

of Madrid flashing by with a steady, solid rhythm—you could get a taxi to any point in the city for the equivalent of a quarter—he lit another cigarette, exhaled slowly, decided he wouldn't say anything to them about it. Nothing. *Nada*. Some things deserve to remain private.

Jersey Shore

Stories ... Stephen Crane wrote a great short story of the Great Plains, the endless prairie in the vast middle of America, in which there is a character "The Swede," Fitzgerald wrote of "the lost Swede towns." A harsh environment—brutal in winter and summer, only a couple months in the year when there is a chance of good weather. The great vistas stretching to the far, far flat horizon, day and night. Flatness. And the endless winds—Loren Eisley thought the constant moan of it, in western Nebraska, drove his mother mad. People once lived in sod houses there.

The Southwest is different. New Mexico, Arizona, Colorado, west Texas even. Some of the cities in that area are grim to think on—Amarillo, Odessa, Wichita Falls, Oklahoma City, Tulsa. There are odd, anomalous things found—a *James Joyce Center* at the University of Tulsa, for example. Oil money? Joyce would probably be amused. Ten Cadillacs, buried in a row, fins up out of the earth, twenty miles from Amarillo. And a steak house, where a one-hundred and ten pound woman holds the record of eating a steak weighing more than four pounds. Then there is Marfa, Texas. Who has been to Marfa?

In Bradford, Pennsylvania, surely one of the most remote outposts—"the icebox of Pennsylvania"—two miles from the New York state line, there are working oil wells in the very center of the town, weekly jet flights to Dallas, and a yearly gathering, in the nearby Allegheny National Forest, of the Pagans, a feared East Coast biker club, corollary to the West Coast's notorious Hell's Angels, and Los Angeles' Satan's Slaves. Perhaps the oddest sight in Bradford is the Zippo Lighter Factory, on the front of which a three-story Zippo Lighter is outlined in neon. Throughout the night, its square top flips open, a neon flame ignites, and the top closes again. Pennsylvania, for some reason, has many oddities. Hunter S. Thompson once lived and worked as a reporter, in Jersey Shore, PA—at least two hundred miles from the Jersey Shore.

Whitman's grave is in Camden, derelict now like a bombed Chechen city, or Detroit. Grant's Tomb is in New York City, Lindbergh's leather flying helmet in a small town in north-central Pennsylvania, and George Washington's formidable-looking false teeth at Mt. Vernon, on the Potomac, across which, legend has it, he once threw a coin, or a stone.

And in DeKalb, Illinois—for which a very popular brand of hybrid corn is named—there is a museum of barbed wire in the mansion home of the inventor, a friend of Bet-A-Million Gates.

Burmese Cuisine

So this is the way it was. Went out and bought a Cross ballpoint refill for a pen my sister gave me many years ago. One of many gifts, over years. It didn't fit, didn't work, although the sales clerk had announced, with a flourish, "We have a match!" Somebody in the shop said , the way you overhear things, "I'll tell you one thing—you won't get rotten lettuce in Burmese food."

And I realized I know nothing about Burmese cuisine. A melding of Thai, Indian, Cambodian, Vietnamese, and Chinese. Every day, or so it seems, I go by the Mandalay, whose sign reads "Burmese Cuisine." And it is here I partake of a dish called "Rangoon Beef." It has much garlic in it, and this can cause complaints, reminding me of the anecdote a friend told of a famous math professor at UC Berkeley. He did not like to meet with his students in his office, but this was required; a minimum of office hours had to be kept. So he ate raw garlic in his office. Few assayed a meeting with him.

Burmese cuisine was like San Francisco, after all. Anything was possible. An eight hundred and ninety five dollar bottle of Desai sake was possible, in a restaurant that gave a view of the twinkling Bay Bridge. Maybe the city of Saint Francis had always been thus. It could be intoxicating. You could live like that for years. That was the problem. If you walked on The Embarcadero late at night, in the soft fog, there was a real sense of longshoremen, stevedores, dock workers, merchant sailors' voices coming out of narrow, dimly lit bars. Nobody could disprove that.

A student once gave me a Waterford pen. "To write with," he said. I have the pen, but I have kept it in its stout blue case. Every once in a while I look at it, remember the student, think of his kindness. Wonder where he is, what life's brought him. What road is he on now? When you live in a city, I think it's more often than not—even with all the social media tools—that you lose touch. You lose touch. You are always trying to get it back. Authenticity.

But there is that "Rangoon Beef."

Mahoney's Café

Nobody actually ate at Mahoney's Café. At least it wasn't much noticed, if anyone did. You didn't need to be inside Mahoney's for long to forget food. The overwhelming scents were stale, spilled cheap beer, disinfectant from the toilet in back (where few ventured), and the still-there remnants of cigarette smoke, cheap department store perfume, malodorous sweat of various stripes, and a sharp, rank, feral odor at points. It wasn't an atmosphere that inclined one's thoughts to dining, or even eating.

On the scarred, cigarette-burnt wood bar sat a tall glass jar of deviled eggs, packed in a carmine broth. No one had ever seen anyone eat one of these. Several varieties of beef jerky were available via a vending machine. For those who actually ventured into the toilet—"Rest Room," a blue neon sign indicated—another machine dispensed a selection of condoms, including the famous "French Tickler," and in a rainbow spectrum of colors. Far at the rear was the grille, where sizzleings erupted from time to time, shouted imprecations, occasionally a crash of crockery, dishes. The cry "Burgers workin!" would be heard. Who ate these? You did not want to know.

The qualifications for tending bar at Mahoney's were mysterious. The drinks were not bad, but neither were they good. The offered beers were the same, mediocre. No one drank wine there, although there were some dusty bottles displayed behind the bar. It was not really a place where one went to drink. Some said it was a "fight" bar, and it was true that nasty street-type fights took place in a closed-in space in a small dead-end of a street, out back. There, someone could jack someone else's jaw good, get up in their face, fix them so they wouldn't forget it. A girl in Mahoney's once asked him if he'd ever been in a fist-fight, and when he replied "No," she nodded, and said "I didn't think so." Women found here invariably smoked heavily.

People who went here were later noted in the newspaper to have been found by the Magistrate "Unfit for Arraignment." A local, who lived just down the street, made a sign "Unfit For Arraignment" and stuck it in his lawn. It was torn down, thrown on his porch.

An odd architectural feature of the establishment was the three concrete steps one mounted to actually enter the bar's dark green front door. He had seen, in winter when these steps would ice over, men slip, sprawl sideways to the street, falling heavily, cursing. "Goddamn... goddamn sunavabitch!" It reminded him of the scene in Dreiser's *Sister Carrie*, where Hurstwood sprawls in the dirty slush of a Manhattan street, cursing.

There was a sign behind the bar at Mahoney's. It read "This is a place where people seek the truth. And find it."

Disappearing

Art Pepper, near the end of his life, playing at The Great American Music Hall, in San Francisco. With a trio of veteran Los Angeles sidemen, a disappearing breed. Like him. An alumnus of San Quentin, one-night gigs, traveling on a bus. A bus.

He quips, between numbers, about Patty Hearst, looking out from the small stage.

"Patty Hearst. She's cool. Tania. SLA… what can you say?"

Trenchant.

Straight life, which is what he finishes then with. "Straight Life."

Outside, it's full night. A young man slumped in a familiar slouch at the corner of Larkin and Bush. A very light rain polishes the street, the neon gleams cold. Up on the third floor of a flaking apartment building that was probably quite a place in the forties, fifties, a woman looks down, then pulls the drape shut.

You find that you can still hear that music, even though it's gone.

Gone.

With Nietzsche, In the Diner of the Midwest

Huey Newton, Great Helmsman, died on an anonymous street in West Oakland, on a mild night. Shot. What was Trotsky's last meal? Whatever it was, he died with an ice pick driven into his head.

Deer hunters gathered at a rural diner in Michigan, dead deer tied to their truck fronts, or roofs. This tavern had a famous collection of trophy buck heads. And famous Christmas decorations.

Run Over

He had the misfortune. Run over by a black Maserati (owned by a hot local chef) in the outer reaches of Lake Street. A pricey enclave these days, even some billionaires. Some "corporate" houses. Some places lived in most of the year by Dobermans. Some only a couple of weeks a year, at Christmas.

So maybe it was bound to happen. The Fitzgeraldian haunts of Fame.

Famous, Famous

By the hand-built stone fireplace in the old farmhouse living room (with tall, old glass windows) we sat in a circle and read poems. One each, going around like that. Several children watched attentively—their amazing faces, every child's face so, lit by the fire. Had anyone driven by on the deep-rutted old dirt road, they'd have seen the beam of the tall, lighted windows, the pulse of the fire. Snow, beginning to fall.

DON SKILES is the author of *Miss America and Other Stories*, *The James Dean Jacket Story*, *Rain After Midnight*, and the novel *Football*. His work has appeared in *Quaartsiluni*, *Snowmonkey*, *Silenced Press*, *Over the Transom*, *Mung-Being*, and *Chicago Quarterly Review*.

His poetry appears in three books from Viking Dog Press/Conehenge Studios (with the work of painter Claribel Cone): *18 Views of San Francisco*, *Sono Choushi!* and *Blue Rhapsody*.

CPSIA information can be obtained
at www.ICGtesting.com
Printed in the USA
FSHW010636140120
66051FS